MERMAID SONG

A FAIRYTALE COLLECTION

ANTHEA SHARP

Fiddlehead Press

Want to make sure you hear about Anthea's new books? Join her newsletter,
and get a *free* short story when you sign up! Find out more at
www.antheasharp.com

Cover by Ravven

Professional editing by LHTemple. Copyediting by Editing720.

ISBN: 9781680130508

QUALITY CONTROL: We care about producing error-free books. If you
discover a typo or formatting issue, please contact antheasharp@hotmail so
that it may be corrected.

CONTENTS

Dedicated to all you lifelong fairytale readers ~ magic awaits.

ABOUT THE STORIES

Mistress Bootsi
A girl sets out to seek her fortune - and luckily, she has a clever cat for a companion, in this *Puss in Boots* retelling.

The Sea King's Daughter
The Little Mermaid, reimagined in an ancient Celtic setting full of wild and bittersweet magic.

Faerie Song
A magical retelling of the *Pied Piper*, with a dark faerie twist.

Escape: A Liza Roth Adventure
A princess on the run and her feline companion find adventure and danger on Starhub Station in this story based on the Icelandic fairy tale *Kisa the Cat*.

Waltzed
A Victorian *Cinderella* retelling complete with an absent-

minded Godmother, an orange carriage, and a slipper mishap. Prepare to be swept away into this (nonmagical) fairytale romance.

MISTRESS BOOTSI

THERE ARE tales that begin *Once upon a time*, and I suppose that is a fine enough start for my own story, though I am not, perhaps, the usual sort of hero. I am not a knight, or sorceress, or princess in disguise, but merely a cat.

Very well, there is nothing *mere* about the feline state, I'll grant you that. And yes, I imagine you might be surprised that I can speak. My great-grandmother was a *Cait Sidhe* who strayed into the mortal world and decided to remain, and her offspring have been part of the Miller family ever since—though I'm the last of them, it seems. My kittens, so far, are all of the normal, non-speaking variety of cat, with so little faerie blood as to make no difference. My own fault, I suppose, for choosing that strong, stupid Tom... but that is not *this* tale.

As a youngling, my mother warned our litter to be careful with our talents. Humans are strange, untrusting things, and she made us swear to only reveal our abilities in great need, and only to those whom we could trust beyond a doubt.

Many of my brothers and sisters, in fact, never spoke a

word in their lives. But I did, and soon enough you'll understand why.

When I was scarcely full grown, father and mother Miller decided to leave their lives as flour-grinders and retire to the warm southlands. After selling what they could, they divided their remaining possessions among their children. The oldest inherited the mill, which he was most pleased about, having the inclination to continue the family business. The middle daughter received the horses in the stables, and she was glad to add them as breeding stock to her own fine herd.

And the youngest daughter? Well, Elisetta had ever craved adventure, and I thought it a fine thing to be bequeathed into her care. Elly always knew precisely where to scratch behind my ears and under my chin, and she'd smuggled more than one dish of cream to me, when her parents weren't looking.

One bright summer morning, the parents bid farewell to their offspring. My own mama groomed me one last time (though I was certainly too old for it) and told me to take good care of myself, cautioning me once more to be careful with my secrets.

I purred and butted her head with my own, and reminded her not to worry. My last sight of her and my older brother was the two of them curled up in the bed of the cart, content in the sunshine, as the Millers drove off.

Elly's siblings had each offered to house her and give her work, but she declined. Instead, she prepared to take to the road herself, to see what adventures lay in store. I was happy to join her, especially as she'd devised a comfortable sling to carry me in.

In addition to myself, Elly carried a pack with some provisions and changes of clothing, and a pouch worn next to her skin with a few silver and copper coins.

As she was a strapping lass, and I a small cat and not too much of a burden, we made good progress. Soon we'd left the village behind and were striding briskly along toward the capital, where Elly hoped to make her fortune.

"I'm a good worker," she told me, though she didn't yet realize I could understand her, and reply if I chose. "I'm clever with my hands. I'd wager I can save up enough for a house of my own some day, if I find the right profession."

I simply purred up at her and nudged her fingers, hoping she'd pet me under the chin again.

"I know I don't want to grind flour, or tend horses, at any rate," she said, absently petting me. "And maybe I should keep going. Take a ship and see the entire world!"

I gave a short, unhappy meow to that. The idea of being surrounded by water was not particularly appealing, even if it meant plenty of fish to eat. I was much more fond of staying dry than I was of a fresh piece of salmon.

Elly laughed. "Why, Bootsi, sometimes I almost think you can understand me. What a funny cat you are."

I kept myself from making any reply, but merely settled down more comfortably in the sling, and soon fell asleep.

It took us several days to reach the city. Elly and I bedded down in a number of barns, where I was happy to catch mice (I've always been a most excellent hunter). Elly did a bit of work in return for supper, a place to sleep, and breakfast the next morning. The farmwives were generous with their provisions, and we never went hungry at lunch.

One afternoon we crested a hill, and Elly halted.

"There it is," she said, her voice hushed with wonder. "The city."

I peeked over the edge of the sling, then blinked to see so many buildings spread out over a green valley. Not all of them were simple one and two stories, either. There were towers and steeples, turrets and minarets jutting into the sky. The sea winked, flat and silver, beyond.

I was not altogether certain coming to the capital was a good idea.

But Elly, with a little skip to her step, started down the hill. I had no plans to abandon her, and so I was carried along with her into the noisy, smelly city.

At first it was not so bad, but the deeper we went into the streets, the more uncomfortable I became. The stink of humans made my whiskers twitch, but the dogs were even worse—leaping and barking until my nerves quivered.

A few other cats slunk about the alleys, hissing when they caught sight of me. I felt very young and untried, and could tell by the slowing of Elly's steps that she felt the same. The sun was starting to go down, and so much of the sky was covered by tall buildings that darkness fell very quickly.

The crowds we'd been traveling though dissipated as the city dwellers made their way home, and a cold wind blew in off the water.

"Surely there's somewhere we can stay the night," Elly said, glancing about the nearly empty street. "Perhaps I'll ask that fellow there."

I gave a little meow of warning, but she paid me no heed as she strode toward the rough-looking man leaning against a nearby wall.

"Pardon me," Elly called. "Do you know where a weary traveler might spend the night?"

The man looked her up and down. "Have ye any coin?"

"A small bit," Elly admitted, which I thought was rather unwise.

He uncrossed his arms and took a step forward, and I did not at all like the way he regarded my human.

"Give it over, then," he said.

"I don't think so." Elly backed away, one arm protectively around me.

The fellow lunged, and Elly whirled, darting away between two of the nearby buildings. She pelted down the alley, jolting me up and down, while I thought furiously of a way to save us.

"Oh no!" she cried, fetching up against a brick wall enclosing the alley.

I looked up at it. Too high for her to climb, certainly. The man chasing us let out an unpleasant chuckle.

Quickly, she scooped me out of the sling and set me on my feet. "Run, Bootsi."

I darted away, but only to the cover of a pile of nearby crates. As the man stepped down the alley toward Elly, I summoned my deepest, harshest voice.

"What's that sound?" I yelled.

Our pursuer hesitated and glanced over his shoulder.

"Hand me my club," I continued. "There's someone outside. I'll give him a beating."

Then I leaped upon the crates, sending them tumbling down with a clatter.

That was enough to send the man running back down the alley, and I watched him go, lashing my tail.

"Who's there?" Elly said softly, peering into the shadows.

"It's me," I said. "Bootsi."

To her credit, she only hesitated a moment before catching me up into her arms. "You can talk?"

"Yes. And now, we'd best find another place to be, in case that fellow returns."

Shaking her head with wonder, Elly tucked me back into the sling and we crept out of the alley. There was no sign of the man who'd chased us, but Elly used much caution until we'd returned to a busier part of the city.

A night market took up most of an enclosed square. Elly and I wandered through, and I could not help drooling a bit at the delicious scent of meat and fish. To my delight, Elly paused beside a vendor selling skewers of meat and hot potatoes, and handed over a few coppers for our dinner.

"Excuse me," she asked the cook, an older woman with gray hair tucked under a kerchief. "Do you know where we might spend the night in safety?"

The old woman frowned at her. "The city isn't safe, my dear. Don't you know that? An ogre has taken up residence in the castle and imprisoned the royal family. You'd best leave while you can."

Elly glanced at the crowds around us. "Why is everyone else here, then, if it's as dangerous as you say?"

"We're city dwellers. Where else will we go?" The woman shook her head. "Some have taken ship, a few others gone into the country, but the rest of us suffer here, and wait."

"Wait for what?" Elly asked.

"Why, for someone to come free the king and his family! Someone will, mark my words. In the last fortnight, at least ten heroes have gone into the castle to challenge the ogre."

"What happened to them?" Elly's eyes were wide.

"The ogre ate them. He'll eat you too, if you stand about in the streets much longer."

With that, the old woman began closing up her cart. I glanced around, to see that the rest of the vendors were doing the same.

"It's late," Elly said. "Might you have a place by the fire where I could spend the night? I'll leave first thing in the morning, I promise."

The old woman wrinkled her nose, but reluctantly agreed that Elly and I could sleep beside her hearth. She led us back to her small house and shared a bit of turnip soup with us for supper, during which time she told Elly how the ogre had come to the city.

"He can change himself into all manner of creatures," the woman said. "As a scaly dragon, he charged the castle walls, and they couldn't stand against him. He commandeered the army, and has got a force of soldiers guarding the castle now. Perhaps he's not an ogre at all, but a wicked sorcerer."

After supper, Elly curled up in a blanket beside the hearth and was soon fast asleep. I, however, lay awake in the dim, smoky hours, staring at the banked coals in the fireplace and devising a plan.

As soon as Elly stirred in the morning, I climbed on the blanket and butted her chin with my head.

"Wake up," I said quietly. "We're going to the castle today, to slay the ogre."

"What?" She blinked at me.

"As I told you." I nudged her fingers until she began to pet me. "All we need to do is get inside the walls. Leave the rest to me."

She did not argue, or insist we run away from the city, and I was proud to have a human who displayed such bravery. And one who was willing to listen to me.

Elly insisted on giving the old woman a silver coin for her hospitality as we bid her farewell.

"After all," Elly said as we stepped up the street, "either tonight I'll have saved the castle or I'll be eaten by the ogre. Either way, one coin won't make the difference."

I purred loudly to show my approval.

The nearer we got to the castle, the more empty buildings we saw. Those nobles who could, had fled, and everyone else living near the walls had moved further away. No one wanted to be the ogre's next snack.

Elly walked boldly up to the castle gates, with me peeking out of the sling. The guardsmen watched us with suspicious eyes, hands clenched around their pikes and sword hilts.

"Halt!" cried the soldier guarding the small postern door. "State your business and show your weapons."

"I have no weapons," Elly said. "I'm here to provide amusement for the ogre by showing him my dancing cat."

I extended my claws at that, pricking my human's skin. But it was too late for her to unsay the words.

"Dancing cat?" The guard squinted. "Show us."

The nearby soldiers converged as Elly brought me out of the sling. She set me on the cobbles, whispering a quick apology. I glared at her and lashed my tail, but there was nothing else I could do. We must enter the castle and be granted an audience with the ogre if my plan was going to work.

"Well?" the guard asked. "Seems like just an ordinary cat."

With an inward sigh, I leaped into the air and performed a graceful turn. I landed on all fours, and wove to the left and the right, then spun about once more. As a final move, I crossed my paws and bowed before the guard at the door.

The soldiers clapped.

"That is a good trick," the guard said. "We'll let you in, but you still have to surrender any weapons."

Elly handed over her belt knife, which hardly qualified as a weapon. Certainly it was no threat to the ogre. The blade was scarcely sharp enough to cut slices of fruit.

"If I were a hero come to challenge the ogre," she asked, "would I be allowed to bring a sword?"

"You, a hero?" The guard laughed at her. "You're nearly as funny as your cat, girl."

She set her mouth, but luckily did not argue with the man. Instead she scooped me up and stalked through the postern door without a word. I thought of hissing at the guard as we passed, but thought better of it. He might take offense and change his mind about letting us into the castle, and then my foolish display of dancing would have been for naught.

Once through the wall, a servant in red and black livery escorted us across the courtyard and into the castle's great hall. The air smelled harsh, with the tang of something I knew was dark magic, though I'd never encountered such a scent before.

The ceiling rose far overhead and the room echoed eerily, as though the empty space was used to being filled by a bright mob of courtiers and visitors. Instead it was uncomfortably quiet.

Elly's steps faltered as the servant led us across the expanse of marble floor toward the dais at the end of the hall. A hulking figure sat there, on a throne made of bone and shadow—easily three times the size of the king's old throne, which lay on its side behind the dais, as if discarded.

"Courage," I whispered to my human.

She gave me a gentle pat, and I felt her shoulders straighten.

"Who comes?" the figure asked in a booming voice.

"Put me down." I wriggled in the sling

Elly took me out and set me gently on the floor. The stone was cold beneath my paws. I walked forward until I was a short leap from the throne. The fetid smell of ogre sweat pinched my nose, and I could hear the breath rasping in and out of his throat. One of his hands was big enough to crush me, should he so choose.

"Your eminence." I made the ogre a bow. "My name is Mistress Bootsi, and I have come to look upon your might."

"A talking cat?" He laughed, a harsh, nasty sound. "If you thought I'd be impressed, I'm not. I have no use for you."

The ogre stood and, in a wink, transformed to a huge lion. He roared, and I shivered in fear. My instincts clamored for me to run, *run*! It took all my courage to stand my ground, and I hoped that Elly had the sense to do the same. Being breakfast for a lion was not part of my plan.

A heartbeat later, the ogre returned to his original form.

"You see?" He gave me an ugly smile, his teeth very white, and very sharp. "I can become a mighty cat, should I feel the need."

"That was most impressive," I said. "Of course, an ogre of your great stature can turn into anything large and intimidating. Such things must come easily to you."

"Of course they do." His reddish eyes narrowed.

"I wonder if you…" I shook my head and sat back on my haunches. "Ah, never mind."

"If I what?" he growled.

"It was a passing notion. I simply don't see how you could become anything small and unthreatening." I looked up at him, my eyes wide.

His wide face furrowed in a frown. "Of course I can!"

A moment later, a dog stood upon the dais. It barked at me. Once more, I had to restrain my urge to flee.

With a whooshing sound, the ogre changed back.

"You see?" He scowled at me. "I can become anything I like."

"As you say." To hide my trembling, I began to lick my paw. "Although…"

"Although what?" The ogre was clearly becoming impatient with my dangerous game. His huge hands clenched and unclenched.

"Some might say a large dog is still a representation of your inner strength, Lord Ogre. Which, of course, is tremendous. I can see why changing into something small and harmless, like a mouse, is beyond your power."

"What?" he cried. "Nothing is beyond my power!"

He raised his fists, his complexion turning orange with effort. The lamps fixed to the walls vibrated, and small chips of marble skittered across the floor as the very foundations of the castle shook.

A second later, the ogre was gone. A small gray mouse stood on the dais, whiskers twitching. It was the moment I'd been waiting for.

Quick as quick, I pounced, sharp claws unsheathed.

The mouse squeaked and darted for cover, but I caught it

and—despite my desire to toy with it—bit it right at the back of the head.

It slumped, a quiver running through its body. Perhaps it was attempting to change back into an ogre. I held it down with one paw and bit again, my sharp teeth making quick work of the mouse. It tasted sour, but, just in case, I ate it up, every scrap.

"Bootsi!" Elly cried, running over to me. "You did it—you defeated the ogre."

She made a face at the smear of mouse blood on the floor, but that didn't stop her from scooping me up in her arms. I purred mightily, quite pleased with myself.

"There she is," a voice cried.

Elly turned, to see a gray-haired man in a tattered robe step through the door behind the dais. He was accompanied by a tall, dark-haired young man, and a half dozen soldiers.

"Bow to your king," one of the soldiers said to Elly.

"Your highness?" Elly blinked in confusion, then made a bow—somewhat awkward, due to the fact that she was holding a cat.

"Rise," the king said. Despite his disheveled appearance, his voice was regal. "You have saved my kingdom from the ogre, young lady. Any reward you desire is yours for the asking. Gold, a castle of your own, my son's hand in marriage."

"Um." She glanced down at me. "I don't really want a castle, and while your son is very handsome…" She blushed at the words, then hurriedly continued. "Actually, it was my cat, Bootsi, who killed the ogre."

The king's brows rose. "Are you certain you don't want to take credit? That's rather unusual in these types of circumstances. The cat belongs to you, after all."

My tail lashed twice at that comment, but I knew that Elly would defend me—as she did.

"Cats belong to no one, your highness." Elly looked up at the king. "I think some gold might come in handy, though, and perhaps a little cottage somewhere—not too close to the city, but not too far away. Would you like that, Bootsi?"

I purred loudly to show my approval, choosing not to reveal my ability to speak. I did not trust kings much more than I trusted ogres. If the monarch discovered I was a magical cat, well, he might decide to take me for himself.

"Miss…" The prince stepped forward. "What is your name?"

I liked the kindness in his eyes, and the fact that he was the only one who bothered asking Elly who she was.

"I'm Elisetta Miller," she said. "And you must be Prince Marcus."

"I am." He gave her a smile. "Once you're settled in your new cottage, might I come pay you a visit?"

I purred again, liking how polite this prince was. Perhaps he and Elly would make a match, and she'd end up with the prince and the castle after all.

And, as you know, she did just that. You're proof of that, little one, though I'm not sure how much you understand of my tale. Baby humans are such strange, incompetent things. Why, you can't even crawl about!

Elly tells me that will come, eventually. I trust I'll be here to see the day. And who knows, perhaps I'll find a better mate next time, and you'll have a talking kitten for a companion of your own.

Whatever the case, the world holds adventures aplenty for you, youngling. Yes, grin that drooling smile at me. But as you grow up, I know you will have the courage to face ogres and the generosity to share your rewards.

And, most of all, the wisdom to listen to your cat.

AUTHOR'S NOTE

This story was inspired by the fairytale *Puss in Boots*, also known as *The Master Cat*. I love the idea of a clever talking cat —and her companion, who has the sense to listen to her advice. Bootsi is based on Zella, a sometimes silly, sometimes sensible feline who shares our house. She is a mighty hunter and, if she could talk, would certainly be clever enough to trick and devour an ogre.

If you liked this story, please look for my other work. You might enjoy my collection of magical short stories: Tales of Feyland & Faerie. Also, The First Adventure, the prequel novella to my bestselling Feyland series, is FREE at all retailers. You can sign up for my newsletter as well, and get a bonus story in return. Thank you for reading!

THE SEA KING'S DAUGHTER

THE SURFACE of the North Sea rolled and ruffled quietly beneath the May wind. In the sky overhead, gulls caught the eddies, calling in high, lonely voices. The rocky shore of Eire rose on the horizon, a dark blur of land before the water stretched away for thousands of miles to the west.

Beneath the waters, the calm beauty of the day mattered little. Pale sunshine filtered down, and further down, to the very halls of the Sea King, where the matters of the world above meant very little. His palace rose from the sea bed, whorls of shell and pearl glowing with iridescence. Four fanciful towers, one for each of his daughters, were decked with banners of woven sea grass that waved in the gentle eddies

The open, curved halls were traversed by fishes and merfolk alike on their way to the throne room for the birthday celebrations of the king's youngest daughter, Muireen.

This was not any birthday, however, but the coming of age Muireen had been waiting years for. Finally she was turning seventeen and would be allowed to rise to the surface for her first glimpse of the mortal world.

Six years earlier, her eldest sister Aila had been the first of them to break the surface of the bright water and see what wonders the world above held.

"Tell us, tell us," her sisters had clamored when she returned, then listened, wide-eyed, to Aila's descriptions of the wheeling birds, the bright sun, the taste of air in her lungs instead of water.

She had even glimpsed a mortal ship riding majestic over the waves, all unaware of the kingdom they traveled over. Although her bodyguard had not allowed her swim any closer, for fear of discovery, Aila had heard singing, and a strange buzzing instrument not known beneath the sea.

The next sister to rise, Dagmar, had shaken her head dismissively upon her return.

"It's gray and cold," she'd said. "Water spits in cold drops from the sky, and the bones of fish float, rotting, in the waves. There is no reason to visit the world above."

"What of the mortals?" Muireen had asked.

"I saw no sign," Dagmar said, flat disinterest in her voice.

When the second-youngest sister made her trip to the surface, she proclaimed it "quiet and a bit boring."

Privately, Muireen vowed that she would swim toward shore. She would stay from dawn to dusk and do everything she could to catch a glimpse of the mortals who inhabited the world of air. Whether or not the guards that would accompany her would allow such a thing was a question she pushed away. Her determination was strong enough to succeed.

For years, Muireen and her sisters had scavenged the shipwrecks scattered on the ocean floor. But while her older siblings had lost interest, Muireen still was fascinated by the strange objects to be found in the detritus. She could not make heads nor tails of many of the items, but whether they were weapons or decorations or strange tools, they piqued her imagination.

"Why can we not visit the surface more than once a year?" she'd asked her father. "Surely we can learn things from the mortals above."

"No," the Sea King had said, his voice hard. "The only thing they may teach our kind is death and destruction. Our history is filled with tales of murder, the blood of our people staining the currents while they hunted us down without mercy. Once a year is danger enough."

Only the weight of law and custom kept her father from forbidding all merfolk from ever rising to the surface.

Today, though, was her day. Muireen's heart beat faster. Today, she would feel the mystery of the sun on her face, breathe the strangeness of air, hear the sounds of the birds.

And maybe, if luck was with her, she would set her eyes on a mortal.

EIRIC AIRGEAD SET his carefully folded nets in his small boat, checked that it was not taking on water, then stepped in and pushed off from the stone jetty. The sky overhead cupped the pearly pre-dawn light, and the village's small harbor was busy with fishermen heading out to make the day's catch. Half the fleet was already gone, their boats patches of darkness over the pewter water.

The sea wind blew Eiric's dark hair about his face, the

breeze strong enough for him to raise sail. Quickly, his boat flew out, rocking up and down when he hit the rougher water outside the sheltering curve of the harbor. Behind him, white-washed cottages glowed softly with the dawn over their shoulders. The stone-walled fields and lanes climbed up the hillside, and he could see a half dozen villagers striding up to tend the fields and flocks.

He'd never had the heart of a farmer, himself. The sea always called to him, the waves whispering his name. The village lived by the sea. And died by it, as well—as no doubt would be his own fate.

But while he lived, he'd ride his small boat over the waves, casting his nets beneath the surface to pull up silver shimmering wonders of fishes. He'd sing, and play the tin whistle tucked in his pocket to pass the time. Most of all, he'd know the freedom of the wind and water, the language of current and cloud.

Bright porpoises danced beside his boat, and seals watched him with their large, dark eyes. The huge *Ainmhí Sheoil* moved like a dark shadow below him, but he was wiser than to cast a line for the shark. His boat was too small, his arms too weak.

It took many men in a larger craft to be able to ride out the death run of such a massive fish. Once, one of the village's boats was gone for nearly an entire moon. When they finally returned, they told a harrowing and heroic tale of being dragged far to the north by the basking shark, at last over-coming it, and then making the long journey home. That winter, the village ate well.

Though Eiric fished alone, he contributed enough to the village's stores that he was considered a hard worker, and a good match for any of the lasses. Red-haired Biddy had made it plain she'd welcome him to come courting, but she had a hard edge that Eiric misliked. Perhaps he might instead woo Orla, who tended her flock of sheep, but she was a quiet girl. Too quiet, mayhap.

Eiric's mother was gone, and his father as well, leaving no one to push him toward a marriage he was not certain he wanted. And so he fished, and played tunes up to the sky, and was content to live alone.

MUIREEN'S SISTERS combed out her hair and braided it with pearls. They burnished the silver-blue scales of her tail until it glowed, and told her she was as beautiful as the sun slanting through the midsummer waves.

When she was finally ready, her sisters accompanied her to the curved-walled, iridescent throne room. There, the king and all the court had assembled to bid Muireen a safe journey to the surface. After an eternity of toasts and speeches, it was at last time for her departure. The currents swirled, tugging at Muireen's hair and slipping over her scales, whispering *come, come*.

"Don't do anything foolish," her eldest sister said as she embraced Muireen in farewell.

"Princess." An older warrior bowed before Muireen, her silver hair braided tightly against her head. "I am to be your bodyguard today. My name is Ceilp."

"Well met, Ceilp," Muireen said. "And thank you for your escort."

The Sea King beckoned, and she went obediently to float before him. *Soon. So soon.*

"Daughter." The king's strong voice sent ripples through the water surrounding them. "Today you will breathe air for the first time and claim your birthright between the worlds. I call upon the blessing of the sun and moon to protect you. I command the tides and currents to carry you safely to the world above, and back home to us. Go now, and see, but take care not to be seen in return. The safety of our people rests in concealment and caution. Do you understand?"

"Yes, Father." Muireen dipped her head in consent, but she could not contain the racing of her pulse.

Of course she would be careful, but she would not return until she'd at least glimpsed a mortal. She'd waited her entire life to visit the surface.

The king lifted his scepter made of glimmering shells.

"Safe travels to you Muireen, daughter of the sea," he said. "And to you, warrior Ceilp."

The merfolk and water creatures let out a liquid cheer. Muireen clasped her finned fingers together and bowed to her father. Her escort bowed even lower, and finally they were free to go.

It took all Muireen's control to keep herself swimming at the sedate pace required by politeness. Although she wanted to give a mighty sweep of her tail to propel her through the pearly opening of the palace gates, the backwash would disrupt the onlookers. Only children and uncouth swimmers sent disruptive wakes when they swam inside the palace. Certainly no princess of the sea would behave so rudely—even though her blood bubbled through her like air, seeking to rise.

Up, up to the brightness above the waves.

When the palace was a glowing shell behind them,

Muireen glanced at her guard.

"Might we swim a bit faster?" she asked, trying to control the impatient twitch of her tailfins.

Ceilp frowned slightly. "Very well. I can see you won't settle until you take your first breath of air."

Muireen didn't hesitate. Stretching her arms ahead of her, fingers spread wide, she thrust her tail up, then down and surged forward. The sea pulled past, strands of kelp waving wildly behind them. Small silver fishes scattered before them and Muireen laughed aloud.

Ceilp kept pace on her right, and though she was not smiling, some joy sparked in her eyes.

Far off and below them the water shaded to indigo, marking the territory of the sea witch. Muireen glanced down and shivered. No one ventured into the witch's domain without a very good reason, and even then such a journey was fraught with peril. She was an unsavory creature who wished nothing but ill upon the mer.

Legend held that once she had been the sea king's lover, but that her ill-humored nature had at last turned him against her. She'd been banished from court and left to dwell in the bitter shadows she preferred, stirring up mischief when she could.

Still, her magic was powerful, and sometimes merfolk in great need turned to her when all other hope was lost.

A shaft of sunlight sifted overhead, lightening the sea to a delicious greeny-blue, and Muireen banished all thought of the sea witch. Today there was no room for dark tales and darker waters. Not when the adventure of a lifetime awaited.

EIRIC FISHED ALL MORNING, his nets yielding a fair catch. When the sun neared its zenith, he pulled out a hunk of brown bread and some dried fish to make a meal. As he finished, brushing the crumbs overboard, the breeze freshened from the west.

He shaded his eyes with one hand and looked to the horizon. Clouds smudged the line between sea and sky, and he frowned. Might be a storm brewing, or mayhap just a squall, but a wise fisherman knew when it was time to head for shore.

Glancing back toward the sheltering bulk of Eire, he realized with a stab of dismay that he'd gone quite a distance from land. Sometimes the currents were tricky out of the north, pushing small boats such as his from their paths and out to sea.

He'd been careless, focused on the good fishing and the sparkle of sunlight on the water and paying little heed to the wind and waves carrying him away. Quickly, he stowed his nets, then wrestled with the sail. The wind was stubborn, changing direction as soon as he'd caught it. The sail luffed, sounding suspiciously like it was laughing at him.

"Hush now," he said, trying to soothe the coarse cloth as well as his own mounting unease. "We'll make it to shore soon enough."

At that, the wind died down entirely. Eiric let out a breath. Why did the elements mock him so?

He didn't want to cast his nets or line back out, in case the breeze freshened. To pass the time, he pulled out his tin whistle, the metal warm from where it had rested inside his coat, and began to play.

Perhaps he could coax the wind to rise if he played something sprightly. Fingers flicking over the holes, Eiric spun the bright notes of a jig into the air. The slap of water against the boat kept an arrhythmic counterpoint but, alas, the sky remained still.

He played another jig, then a reel full of flurries and turns, and then a quieter tune, the melody of an old song about a lover lost at sea. He was not a singer, his voice too rough and low, but with the whistle he could sing out, the notes pure and aching.

Something splashed in the waves behind him.

Eiric turned, halting the music, but there was nothing to be seen except a white froth like lace, already dissolving into the blue green waves. Likely it had been a fish leaping, or perhaps a curious seal, drawn by the sound of his music. Still, that didn't explain the prickling between his shoulder blades.

He waited for several breaths, but whatever it was had gone. Still, he resolved to keep a sharp eye on the water. Fishermen who ignored their instincts went soonest to the bottom of the sea.

"HALT," Ceilp said when Muireen was only a few lengths from the enticing glimmer of the surface.

Impatience surging through her, Muireen did as her escort asked. Overhead, the bottoms of the waves beckoned.

"Why?" she asked.

Ceilp gave her a serious look. "You have never breathed air before. And although our mer magic should make air no different than water, sometimes the transition can be awkward."

"I know," Muireen said. "We must take in a long sip of seawater, then let it out in three quick puffs, then rise to the surface and not breathe in for three heartbeats."

"Indeed." Ceilp said. "Remember it well. Also, it helps to be touching someone who has breathed both air and water. It aids the magic for some reason. Wait." She held out her hand to stay Muireen, who could not seem to keep herself from floating up.

"I will rise first to make sure it is safe," the guard said. "Stay two tail lengths below. Once I determine all is well, rise and take my hand. Then we will break the surface together."

Muireen nodded, her pulse racing like a high tide under the mysterious moon.

With a last, stern look, Ceilp swam up, her tail strokes leaving swirls in the current. After what felt an eon, she descended to where Muireen.

"It is safe," she said. "A storm brews in the distance, but that will not concern us."

She held out her hand, the webs between her fingers a pale orange that echoed the burnished hues of her tail. Muireen folded her fingers around Ceilp's and, tails beating the water, they rose.

In her excitement, Muireen nearly forgot to suck in her seawater and let it out in three pulses. Still, she managed, releasing the last bit of liquid just before the top of her head touched that magical, permeable ceiling where water meets air.

Then her whole face emerged. Conscious of the change in her lungs, she held her breath. Her pulse thundered through her body. Once, twice, thrice. Then she opened her mouth and let the air come in, filling the places that had known only salt and the sea.

The world above the ocean was cool and bright. It felt strange to lose the comforting presence of the water against her skin. Her cheeks and lips and eyes felt bare in a way they never had before, as though something had been peeled away, leaving her exposed.

Her hair was stuck against her head, clinging to her shoulders instead of floating free. And the sounds! Everything was sharp and exciting: the hiss and rush of the water, a high whistling that must be the wind, a distant rumble of surf on stone. The cries of the gulls overhead cut through her.

"Ha!" She could not help her shout of laughter.

"Are you breathing correctly?" Ceilp asked, watching Muireen closely.

"Yes." The word trembled on Muireen's lips. Even her voice was different here, lower and husky-sounding.

"Good." Ceilp released her hand. "Welcome to the world above."

Muireen spun herself in a circle, taking it in. The birds overhead darted and wheeled like fish in the sky. Strange diaphanous whiteness floated higher in the blue. The sun was too strong to look at, the glossy, hard light on the waves enough to make her squint and blink.

"What is that?" She pointed in the direction the sun rose, where a long, dark shape lay low on the horizon.

"Land," Ceilp's said. "The place where humans dwell."

Muireen's new-found breath hitched in excitement. "Can we—"

"No." The older mer's tone was forbidding. "No good comes from anything mortal."

"And what is over there?" Murieen nodded in the opposite direction, where a dark haze filled part of the sky.

"That is the look of a storm blowing in. Fear not; we will be safely below before it arrives."

Muireen frowned. "But I want to see the stars, and the moon, without lengths of water between me and the sky. Surely that is not too much to ask?"

"My duty is to keep you safe, princess." Ceilp emphasized the last word, reminding Muireen of her station, and responsibilities. "For now, you ought to practice changing from breathing air to water, so that your body may become used to the sensation. I will keep watch."

With a sigh, Muireen dove beneath the surface. The water wrapped about her like a blanket, comforting, yet almost smothering. She longed to throw it off, to rise and feel the excitement of air about her once again.

What would it be like, to live as a human, wholly above the surface? To be unable to breathe water, to move about on two ungainly stalks, trapped against the ground?

She would never know.

Instead, she distracted herself with chasing a nearby school of porpoise in and out of the waves. Ceilp even joined in as they leaped and dove. Each time Murieen broke the barrier between water and air, she took in great breaths, tasting salt and cold and, once, a hint of something wild and green blown off the land.

"What is the land called?" she asked Celip, once the guard seemed in a better mood.

"I've heard it is called Eire," Ceilp said.

"Air?" Muireen laughed. "It is a fitting name."

Ceilp shook her head, but there was warmth in her eyes.

"It has a different spelling, and a different nuance on the tongue. It is the name for an ancient goddess of the land, and the mortals have called their home accordingly."

Once again, Muireen glanced at the dark length of the island and silently rolled the name on her tongue. Eire. It seemed a little closer than when she'd first glimpsed it upon the horizon, and she was determined to edge closer still.

After a time the porpoises tired of playing, but under pretext of the chase Muireen had managed to maneuver herself and Ceilp nearer to the land. She sculled idly in the waves, letting the breeze explore her face. Then something tickled the edge of her hearing—a bright, breathy fall of melody that tugged her soul. Music?

"Do you hear that?" She lifted her head. "Oh, Ceilp, might we go a bit closer?"

The older mer set her hands on the two forked daggers belted about her waist, as if to reassure herself of their presence. She glanced up at the sky.

"Music means humans," she said. "It is too dangerous."

"Please?" Muireen tried to keep her yearning from showing in her voice. "We'll be careful. Just—can't we see where it's coming from?"

This was her chance to see a human! She could not turn away from the opportunity.

"No." From Ceilp's tone, there would be no changing her mind.

Muireen shot a regretful glance at the receding porpoises. They would not provide cover any long, which meant she must seize her opportunity now.

Before her guard could guess what she was about, Muireen dipped beneath the waves and sped in the direction the music had come from, using every trick of speed she knew. Behind her, Ceilp called for her to stop, but Muireen ignored the words.

Closer, closer, until she could hear the notes even beneath the waves, wavering and distorted, falling down like tarnished coins. She shivered with delight. Such a sound, made of breath and mystery, was never heard in the sea kingdom. Just ahead, she saw the curved bottom of a small boat, a promise of adventure riding the waves. Barely slowing, she shot up to the surface.

She rose above the waves long enough to glimpse a slender, dark-haired man leaning against the thin mast of his boat, a length of metal held to his lips.

Then Ceilp grabbed her tail and tugged her down with a splash.

"Foolish girl!" The guard glowered at her from the safety beneath the waves. "It's time I took you back to the palace."

"But—"

"No argument."

Under Ceilp's watchful eye, Muireen reluctantly turned her back on the bright glimmer of the world above. Her trick would not work a second time.

As they descended through the waters, the greeny-blue quality of the light seemed darker than before, the liquid murmur of the sea a poor echo of the dancing wind and calling gulls who owned the sky.

She closed her eyes, recalling the face and form of the human she'd seen. His cheeks were burnished bronze by the sun and wind, his dark hair worn short. He had seemed not much older than herself, and she wondered why he was all alone in a boat so far from shore.

"The storm's coming in," Ceilp said. "Feel it in the current? It's best we left the surface when we did,"

Muireen did feel it, the first tremor of turmoil and churn, and her heart squeezed in fear for the fisherman playing his music far above. He was some distance from land, and his craft was so small. But there was no use in begging to return to the surface.

Too late, anyhow—the pearly turrets of the palace rose ahead, glowing with luminescence as the water darkened.

At the entrance to her tower, Muireen pulled a long strand of pearls from her hair and turned to Ceilp.

"Thank you for your escort," she said, handing the guard the pearls. "I will always remember my first journey to the surface."

"It was an honor." Ceilp said. "I am glad no trouble came of it."

"Of course not, with such a capable guard as yourself." Muireen smiled. "I truly am grateful for your service today." Most of all, she was glad of seeing the mortal man. But small fishes had big mouths, and she dared not speak of that encounter. Nothing but trouble would follow if the king knew of it.

"Muireen!" her sister Aila called from the near tower. "You've returned safely! Come and tell us about your first breath of air."

Ceilp made Muireen a formal bow. "I will inform your father that your birthday journey is complete and you've returned safely. Good evening, princess."

"Fine swimming to you," Muireen replied.

As her her guard departed, she glanced up and up. Barely at the edge of her vision, a faint turbulence roiled. The storm.

Her heart clenched at the thought of the fisherman—but her sisters were expecting her. No matter how much she wanted to surge back to the surface, she could not.

At least, not yet.

EIRIC DUCKED his head as another wave crashed against the side of the boat, the harsh spray coating his face and hands. The wind pummeled him, and he reefed the small sail close, trying to control his craft in the face of the raging elements.

Most of the afternoon he'd spent frustratingly becalmed. When he'd tired of playing his whistle he'd turned to mending the nets, though most of his supplies for such were back at his cottage. Still, it passed the time.

Finally, when the sun dipped low, racing its own reflection in the water, the breeze had sprung up. Brisk at first, then brisker still, until Eiric's boat ran before a fierce storm. No matter how nimbly he sailed, his heart clenched within him as the shadow of the clouds overtook the last pewter light shimmering on the sea.

All too soon, he'd been engulfed. Dark gray clouds matched the waves, and he lost all sight of the setting sun. Navigating by instinct, he prayed he was still headed east, and not out over the open waters, where death awaited with outstretched arms.

It took all his skill to keep his boat running upon the backs of the waves, and not directly into their hungry mouths. He did not always succeed. Fingers numb with cold, he fought the storm for what felt like hours. His ears were deafened by the rasp of the wind, his eyes stung nearly blind with salt.

Then he heard it—the crack and smash of waves breaking against stone.

He was near land, but not the sweet cove of the bay beside the village. No, he must have come in to the south where mighty cliffs rose, uncaring that a mortal life would be dashed to nothing against the rocks.

Aye, he'd wanted land. But not like this.

Forcing his hands steady, Eiric wove his boat through the water and wind, fighting to turn aside from the implacable cliffs. Hope strained his lungs as the sound of wave on stone began to fade.

Then he was pitched forward as the boat struck something in the water. Crying out, he grabbed for the side. Missed. A glimpse of black rock, splintered wood, and then the sea closed over his head, cold and relentless.

CHAPTER/scene

MUIREEN WAITED until indigo darkness filled the sea before slipping out of her tower room. The night guards were posted to keep watch for things coming into the palace, not sneaking out. Keeping to the shadows, she swam carefully until she was some distance from the pearly towers.

Then, with powerful sweeps of her tail, she drove herself up to the surface, angling for the place she'd seen the fisherman. The closer she rose to the ceiling of the sea, the more turbulent the water. The bottoms of the waves pulled at her hair and tried to unbalance her, the swirl of storm spinning her about.

Just before breaking into the air, she recalled her training, and prepared her lungs for the transition.

Harsh wind battered her face and shoulders, so much spray in the air that for a dizzying moment her body did not respond. She choked on salt, on the horrible emptiness above the waves. Shuddering, she thrashed her tail, lifting her high enough that her lungs finally responded.

Gasping, Muireen swept her sticky hair from her face and searched desperately for the fisherman's boat. How could he survive such a rage of smacking water and tearing wind?

There was no sign of him.

Surely he'd made for land at the first sign of storm, and was even now safely at home, far from the grasp of the sea. But even as the sensible part of herself argued that she ought to dive down to safety, something else pulled her on, toward the memory of where the island of Eire lay.

At length a strange sound came to her ears, a rhythmic crash and crack. Before she understood it, the storm threw her forward, and she smacked against the side of a rock jutting from the water.

Pain flashed through her, and she ducked down, away from the greedy hands of the weather above. The power of the storm was blunted beneath the water, and she drew in a steadying gulp, searching for calm. She should not be here, where the rocks waited to tear her body.

A bit of wood brushed her arm, borne by the sucking current. Then another.

It took a moment to realize what it meant.

The debris was new and sharp-edged. Some craft had hit the rocks and wrecked. Panic flashing through her, she turned in a circle, every sense alert.

There! Overhead, she saw the remains of a boat smashing up against the stone. And there…

Time slowed.

Muireen's blood beat stronger than the surge of the waves in her ears. She dove, hands outstretched, for the form of the man sinking to his death. It was the fisherman, and for an instant she saw a silver thread stretching from her heart to his, a path of starlight, of fate.

Then she reached him and wrapped her arms about him, pulling them both up, up, driving through the rough water until she reached the harsh air again. He was heavy against her, and cold, his head lolling. The waves beat at them like fists.

Desperately, she swam, steering away from the terrifying crash of sea on stone. Surely the land held more than the hungry rocks. Breath heaving, she scanned the shoreline. There! A bare crescent of sand beckoned, barely wide enough for a single body, framed by jagged black stone. She forced herself forward, her timing and agility slowed by the body in her arms. The tide threw her up against the side of a rock. She twisted, and the stone left a long, painful scrape down her tail.

Then she was through the worst of the surf, and felt the land rise up, pulling away from the sea. Teeth bared, she thrashed forward, for the first time cursing her tail. Ungainly against the rough grains of sand, she pushed the fisherman before her until he was out of reach of the waves.

He was not breathing.

Awkwardly, she turned him on his side and thumped his back.

"Come now, human," she cried. "Spit out the sea and live. Please."

As if hearing her, his body convulsed. A gush of water emitted from his mouth and he shuddered. Muireen laid her hand between his shoulders and willed him to breathe.

Another shiver wracked him. He coughed again, and then she felt the blessed pull of air into his body.

"Yes," she sighed.

His dark hair hid his face and she carefully pushed the sodden strands aside so that she might see his features. His cheeks were pale, but regaining color even as she watched. His lips were too soft for the rest of his face—the sharp nose and stern forehead, the black slashes of his brows.

As she hovered over him, his eyes opened. They were a wild, stormy blue. Muireen stared into those depths, and felt the hook set deep inside her heart.

"You." His voice was a whispered croak. "Saved me."

"Shh," she said. "Rest."

He closed his eyes and lay his head back down on the sand, but still he breathed. Beneath her hand, Muireen could feel his heart beating. Her fisherman would live.

But she refused to leave him alone through the night.

As the water pulled and pushed in and out of the little cove, she held him close and sang him the songs of the sea people in her low, husky voice. The storm quieted, and as the sky cleared she was amazed to see a shimmer of tiny lights overhead—the luminescence of the night that mortals called stars.

After a time, she realized the blackness was fading, nibbled away at one side of the sky by the approaching dawn. She could not stay, could not risk discovery, though it tore her in two to leave her fisherman.

"Farewell," she whispered, bending to lay her lips against

his.

Their breaths mingled, and a salty drop fell from her eye to splash against his cheek. He stirred, and in a sudden panic, Muireen thrashed herself back into the shelter of the sea. The water took her in, cool and welcoming, concealing the secret of her tail.

She hid behind one of the rocks that had battered her. Her body rocked up and down with the now-quiet waves as she peeked out and watched her fisherman lying upon the beach. Watched as he sat up and rubbed at his face, then looked about him like a man who had misplaced something important. Watched as he rose, and winced, and cast a regretful glance at the splintered boards that had washed ashore in the night.

Watched as he turned his back on the sea and trudged away from her into the light of dawn.

CURRENTS of cold water wrapped about Muireen as she swam into the dusky waters of the Sea Witch's domain.

She should not be there, venturing into the clammy kelp beds in pursuit of a vain hope, but for the past week she had been unable to think of anything except her fisherman. The sight of him walking away from her haunted her dreams, and her waking hours, until she could barely eat or carry on a conversation.

It will pass, Muireen told herself, but every day was worse than the one before. She could not help remembering the silver thread she'd glimpsed, tying them together. Was this the reason she could scarcely sleep?

A low moaning sound reached her ears, like the call of a whale, but full of menace, not melancholy. She shivered and swam on, toward a blot of darkness visible ahead.

The blackness resolved to a cave mouth. Muireen halted, her hair drifting about her. It was not too late to turn back.

Oh, but it was. The moment she'd glimpsed the fisherman, it had been too late.

With a steadying gulp, she dove forward, into the cave. It was even colder inside the black stone walls, and a faint greenish light emanated from the depths, a tunnel, leading her on. The sound grew louder, vibrating through Muireen's scales, until she could hardly think, let alone swim.

Then she emerged into a cavern, and the noise ceased. The green light illuminated pale fishes with bulbous eyes and a few sickly strands of waterweed growing from the cavern's sides.

But most of all, it showed the Sea Witch floating in the center of the space, her white eyes turned on Muireen. Hideous white eyes, white skin the color of dead things, suckered tentacles waving from her head, instead of hair. Where her tail should have been was only a swirl of blackness, as though a squid had ejected its ink and fled.

I should not have come. Muireen's chest tightened, and she turned to flee. Rough stone greeted her, slimed with the secretions of moon snails. The tunnel she'd traveled down was gone. Panic racing through her, she pivoted to face the witch.

"Sea King's daughter," the witch said, her voice carrying the memory of a thousand shipwrecks, "I am so very pleased to see you. Tell me, why have you come?"

For a fleeting moment, Muireen was tempted to say it was

all a mistake. Tempted to plead that the Sea Witch release her, unharmed, that it had been nothing more than a foolish dare.

But her heart ached where fate bound her to her mortal man. There could be no simple escape from that snare.

"There is a fisherman," she said.

The witch opened her mouth and let out a keening cry of laughter. "Oh yes, yes. One of those. Delicious. Shall I tell you the terms of the bargain?"

"But you don't know what I want," Muireen protested.

The Sea Witch's blank eyes stared at her. "Of course I do. You want to take on the semblance of a mortal girl, so that you might seek out the fisherman you are so foolishly in love with."

"I'm not in love." Even as she spoke the words, though, a part of Muireen hummed in agreement. "How could I be in love with some ungainly human? I am a princess of the sea."

The witch held up a hand, black webs spread between her clawed fingers.

"I can see the strands of fate wrapped about your heart," she said. "You were wise to come to me, for I can give you what you desire. For a price."

"What is the price?" Muireen's lips felt numb, as though she'd swum through the poisoned strands of a jellyfish.

"You must give me your voice," the witch says. "In return, I will be able to transform you into human form—but only for a year and a day. At the end of that time, you will turn back into a mer and re-enter the sea forever."

A year and a day. It was not long enough—yet it was far better than nothing at all.

"I agr—"

"Wait." The Sea Witch smiled, showing rows of serrated

teeth. "When you return to your form, you will come to me to reclaim your voice. And you will give me one more thing—the bitter tears of your desolation. For in such heart-wrenching sorrow lies great power."

Muireen glanced away from the witch's horrifying countenance and thought desperately, but she could see no alternative. Distasteful as the bargain might be, she must take it.

"It seems I have little choice," she said.

"That is truer than all the pearls in the sea," the witch said. "Now, open your mouth and sing your favorite lullaby."

From somewhere, she conjured a glass bottle and held it over her head.

"Sing," she commanded.

Muireen began, and she could almost see her voice disappearing into the bottle. Slowly, the glass turned a translucent silver-blue: the exact hue of her scales. When the song ended, she glanced down to see that her tail was leached to a sickly gray.

Her gasp of dismay was only a breath. When she tried to form words, nothing came out but little bursts of warm water.

"It is done." The witch tucked the bottle away. "Go now, daughter of the Sea King. Rise to the land, and when you exit the sea, your tail will disappear and you will walk upon two legs. Or attempt to." She let out a harsh cackle. "I will look forward to your visit a year and a day hence."

The Sea Witch raised her hands and pushed, and a sudden dark current swept Muireen up. It bore her quickly through the tunnel and past the wavering kelp, through indigo waters to turquoise, and then pale blue.

With one final surge, it pushed her upon the shore—the same small beach where she'd taken her fisherman.

Muireen gasped and coughed, her lungs unprepared for the transition. Then fierce pain gripped her from the waist down. She opened her mouth, but had no voice to scream. She could only watch in mute horror as her tail disappeared, leaving two spindly stalks in its place.

Legs.

That she must learn to walk upon.

FOR FIVE DAYS, Eiric rested in the bed he'd inherited from his parents. The white walls of the cottage wrapped around him, the breeze rustled the thatch overhead, reassuring him that he was safe.

The villagers brought him broth and helped him rise to use the chamber pot. Biddy was there more often than most, but Eiric did not have the energy to turn away. Fevers wrung him, and a thousand aches from being tumbled against the rocks below the cliffs.

"It's a miracle he survived," the people whispered. "He is truly blessed by the gods."

He did not feel blessed, but cursed. Whenever he closed his eyes to rest, which was often, nightmares of the crashing sea sucked him under.

Again and again he fought to turn his boat, heard the sickening crack of the hull on stone, felt the hungry cold grasp of the waves. The only thing that made his dreams bearable was the memory of a young woman's face, looking down at him.

Her eyes were the warm blue of the sea at midday. Her long hair held brightness and shadow, tangled with sea foam.

Her skin was pale, her hands upon his brow cool and welcome.

Each time he woke, Eiric was filled with a pang of loss. Had he imagined her, or had she rescued him from the storm's hunger?

A smaller, more urgent loss pained him as well, and that was the loss of his boat. He would have to go back to using the small leather coracle that had been his first vessel. No more venturing out into the deep deep waters, where the catch was best. No more room to stow his finest nets. He feared it would be a lean winter.

Biddy would feed you, his thoughts offered up.

He could not think of it—not when the pearl-skinned girl haunted his dreams. And his wakings.

A week unspooled past, and Eiric finally woke feeling... not rested, exactly, but well enough to get out of bed and see if anything salvageable had washed ashore in the tiny cove that had saved him.

He took a hunk of bread stuffed with cheese, a skin of water, and a stout walking stick that had belonged to his Da, and set out over the headland. The sun warmed his shoulders and the top of his head, and he felt as though his life might be worth living, after all.

It took him some time to reach the narrow path cutting through the bracken that led to the tiny beach. He'd had to rest often, and twice refilled his water skin from the small stream that crisscrossed his path.

His lunch called to him, but he'd be better off saving it for after he'd visited the shore. A reward for the hike back up the steep trail, which, in truth, he was not looking forward to.

For now, though, gravity aided him and soon the crash of

the waves against the cliffs filled the air. It took all his concentration to keep his feet under him as he made the last descent to the sliver of sand below.

His boots hit the sand and he stood a moment catching his balance and his breath. Then lost them both when he saw he was not alone.

She was there—the maiden who haunted his thoughts, sitting huddled against a rock, facing the sea. Her long hair covered her like a cloak, but she was naked, the pearly skin of her limbs shining in the sun.

Heartbeat thundering in his ears, Eiric glanced about the little cove, looking for her clothing, or her selkie skin, anything that would help him learn what kind of creature she was. For though she appeared mortal, he knew deep in his soul that she was a magical being.

Sensing his presence, she spun awkwardly about and fixed him with her blue, blue eyes.

"Don't be afraid," he said, his voice a hoarse whisper. "I won't harm you, I swear it."

He could not bear it if she fled back into the waves.

To his relief, she gave him a tentative smile and made no move toward the shining water.

"I'm Eiric," he said, little caring that he might be giving his name to a faerie. Even if she were a fey maiden, he feared he'd already lost his heart to her. Anything more was a trifle. "Do you understand me?"

She nodded, and the beauty in her face made him weak at the knees.

"Have you a name you go by?" he asked.

Again she nodded. Then, with a stricken look, she brought her hand up to her throat and shook her head.

"You cannot speak?"

She opened her mouth, but no sound came out.

"Well then." Eiric settled on the sand. "Still, you and I might converse together in other ways."

A quick nod of her head.

"Where have you come from?"

She turned, hair slipping off one pale shoulder, and gestured at the sea. So, it was as he thought.

"Might I call you Muireann? It means 'sea fair' in my language. And you are very fair."

She blushed slightly and dropped her gaze to the sand. Eiric was hard pressed not to stare openly at her nakedness. Instead, he pulled off his shirt and handed it to her.

"You might put this on, if you like."

Giving him a smile as quick as a silver fish, she held the garment up, studying it a moment before pulling it over her head. She had difficulty with the arm holes, and he reached to help her, drawing one fine-boned hand through the sleeve, and then the other.

"You're not used to clothing, I take it."

He was rewarded with another of her darting smiles.

"I think..." He stared at the waves gnashing upon the rocks. "I think you saved me, sea-fair maiden. Was that you?"

In answer, she rose to her knees a bit unsteadily, then cupped his face between her hands. He held very still, as though she were a wild thing he did not want to frighten. Gods, but she was beautiful. And strong, and brave, by all indications.

Softly, she kissed him on the forehead.

Her touch was enough to undo him. Eiric gathered her

into his arms and held her close. Her heart beat fast, and her skin was cool, but not cold.

Gently, quietly, they kissed, and his heart, at last, felt as though it had come home.

∼

MUIREEN COULD SCARCE BELIEVE her luck. Her fisherman had come to seek her out! Joy surged through her in great waves, despite the awkward feel of her new body. And though she could not speak, they understood one another well enough.

She sat, nestled against his side, and marveled at the warmth of his human body. Together, they watched the waves come in, until the tide nibbled at their toes. With a sigh, Eiric turned to look at her.

"The sun's soon to be setting. I suppose you must return to the sea now, fair maid, though my heart weeps at losing you."

She shook her head at him.

"No?" His eyes widened. "Is it possible you might come live with me, and be my bride?"

She hesitated, but there was no way to explain that she must return to the sea in a year's time. That was a dim cloud on the horizon. After all, a year was a very long while.

She answered him with a kiss.

"Then, my love, we'd best away before dark. We can come another time to search for the wreckage of my boat—if any still remains."

She nodded, and let him pull her to her feet. For a moment she tottered, but with his help found her balance. Walking was more difficult, though, and she let out a little hiss of pain when she stubbed her toe on an outcropping.

"Sit here a moment." He guided her to a rock, then bent and took off his foot coverings.

They came in two parts, she was interested to observe. Mortal clothing was very strange.

"I fear my boots will be too large, and trip you further in any case. But my socks will give you some protection."

He held out the cloth wrappings, then helped her don them. They were warm from his body, and smelled rather strongly, but she was glad of the layer between her tender new skin and the ground.

"Now, Muireann, we must climb to the top of the headland and walk a fair bit before reaching my village. Luckily, it will be dark, so we can avoid the worst of the questions until tomorrow. Are you ready?"

She nodded. No matter what difficulties lay ahead, and she was certain there would be many, it would be worth it with her fisherman by her side.

~

A MOON PASSED, and though the villagers still treated Muireen with suspicion, they had come to accept she was there to stay. All except the flame-haired Biddy, who spat and made the sign of protection whenever their paths crossed.

Together, Muireen and Eiric had managed to pull his wrecked boat from the rocks. Paired with another ruined craft, they'd cobbled together an ugly but seaworthy boat that could take the two of them over the waves.

For though Eiric tried to protest, Muireen was determined to go out with him upon the sea. She'd let him fish alone in his small coracle, and helped him gut and salt the fish he returned with, but she refused to waste their precious time by pining on land, waiting for him.

It was an advantage of not being able to speak, that she simply demonstrated her intent with actions. Though he pleaded, Muireen refused to leave her place at the prow of the boat, and so they set out together.

They worked well together, plying the nets and taking in the fish, And if once or twice Muireen spotted the trailing hair of a mer warrior beneath their boat, she was not alarmed.

No doubt her father had been full of wrath when he'd discovered her bargain with the Sea Witch—but such things could not be broken. Instead, it seemed he'd sent his guard to keep watch on her.

In the evenings, Eiric played his whistle as they sat before the fire in their little cottage. Muireen learned how to cook, though she was ever wary of the flames. She learned to sew, and to knit ungainly socks and sweaters that, while not lovely to behold, kept them warm as the night darkened.

After two moons, she was with child.

"Please jump the broom with me," Eiric said. "We should be handfasted. If not for your sake, then for the babe."

Muireen had refused each time he'd spoken of it before. She was far more comfortable going from cottage to sea and back, content in the simple life they'd woven for themselves. Putting herself on display before the villagers made the old fear rise, that they'd see her as a mer creature and kill her on the spot.

But for him, and the little creature now swimming in her belly, she agreed.

The day of the ceremony dawned bright and clear. Eiric

and Muireen broke their fast, and then he turned to her, smiling.

"My love, I'll leave you now to make ready. Orla has kindly agreed to come help you prepare."

They kissed, and then a knock came at the cottage door. Shy, dark-haired Orla stepped in, carrying a dress the color of sea foam at sunrise.

"I brought you this. It's been in my family for two generations. I thought I might be wed in it, but…" She glanced at Eiric, regret in her eyes. "Anyhow, I'd like you to wear it, Muireann."

Muireen brought her hands together and bowed in thanks. It was very generous. Perhaps—the thought stabbed her heart —perhaps in ten months, when she was gone, Orla might take her place.

Or perhaps not. The love between herself and Eiric was a strong, true bond. She feared he might go mad from losing her, which was part of why she'd refused to wed him. But now there was the babe.

Smiling, she set her hand over her belly. At least there would be some part of her remaining when she returned to the sea.

The ceremony was held on the headland, the bright ocean shining beneath. Eiric said the words, and Muireen emphatically nodded her agreement. Together they let the priestess tie a braided cord about their clasped hands, then jumped the broom while the villagers cheered.

That night they feasted on mutton and ale, and Muireen felt, for a small time, part of the human world.

～

DESPITE HER INSISTENCE on going out in the boat with him, the time came when Muireen's belly was too large for her to be of much use. Too, a melancholy had settled in her soul. Only three months remained until she must leave Eiric forever and return to the sea. Ah, and the Sea Witch would reap well her harvest of tears, for already the sorrow of parting felt unbearable.

Eiric attributed her moods to the state of her body, and was ever patient and kind with her. If he feared that the babe growing within her was less than human, he never spoke a word.

She worried, though, with thoughts that kept her awake and fretting into the cold nights. What if the child was born with fins, or a tail? What if she and the baby were cast out, or killed?

Be well, she thought fiercely at the little life inside her. *Be human.*

From one day to the next, spring came upon the land. The days grew longer and a warm wind blew over the sea.

And Muireen bore a baby girl, with no fins or tail, and her father's dark hair.

"We shall call her Brea," her father said, holding her up and smiling bright as the dawn.

Caught between great joy and great sorrow, Muireen smiled at him through her tears, and nodded. Now that her baby, her daughter, was born, she knew the pain of leaving would be doubled.

But for the month that remained to her upon the land, she could not let that shadow fall over her days. So, with great effort, she pushed it away. Instead, she concentrated on all the perfect moments: Eiric's smile and the scent of him, the soft skin of her daughter, the warmth the three of them made, curled up together in their bed.

The moon waned, and went dark, and that night Muireen dreamed of the Sea Witch.

"Tomorrow," the witch said. "Tomorrow you come back to the sea. If you are not in the water's embrace by sunset, your legs will disappear and you will be revealed for what you truly are. And you will be killed for it."

Muireen woke, shivering, and knew the witch spoke truly. Even if Eiric tried to protect her, he would not be able to stand against the villagers. In her mer form she would be too strange, too frightening. They would take her life, and little Brea's as well.

When Eiric woke and made ready to go out to his boat, she caught his arm and shook her head at him. *Don't go.*

"What's this, love?" He gazed down tenderly at her.

She touched her heart, then his, then glanced down at the babe sleeping in her arms. This was their last day together.

"Aye, I love you and our family with all my heart. But I must go out and fish."

She took his arm again, all her sorrow rising in her eyes, and he relented.

"Very well. But only for today."

She gave a small nod. Yes. Only that day—for tomorrow she would be gone forever.

She packed a lunch, put Brea in her sling, and they roved out over the headland. Eiric collected a bouquet of wild-flowers for her, and she kissed him, wishing that she could speak of what was to come.

They ate, drank cool water from the stream, and she led him to the path down to the tiny beach where they'd first met.

The first shadows from the lowering sun began to fall across the land.

"Should we not be returning home?" he asked.

She shook her head and started down the path. How comfortable her legs had become in a year, how deftly she stepped around stones, feeling herself balance upright in the air. Even carrying the small weight of her baby, it seemed a simple thing, to stride across the land.

When they reached the sliver of sand, she sat, facing the ocean.

Eiric settled beside her, one strong arm around her shoulders as she fed Brea for the last time. When the baby was finished, Muireen handed her to her father, her arms aching with loss.

The banners of the clouds were beginning to turn silvery orange. Heart aching, Muireen stood and stripped off her clothing: shawl, blouse, skirts and shoes. She unbraided her hair until it fell loose about her shoulders, brushing her back and belly.

Eiric watched, his gaze solemn.

When she went to her knees before him, a single tear slipped from his eye.

"Ah, beloved." His voice was choked with sorrow. "Is this our end, then? Must you return to the sea and leave me cruelly alone?"

She set her hand on Brea's head, then looked deep into the eyes of her fisherman. *Be strong, for our daughter*, she thought, even as her heart was breaking.

Their lips met. The sun dipped lower, kissing the horizon.

Then Muireen pulled away and flung herself back, into the arms of the sea. Pain ripped through her as her legs cleaved together. She gasped, and in that moment found her voice.

"Remember me, Eiric," she called. "You are my true love."

"As you are mine, sea maid." He rose, cradling their child in his arms. "Will I ever see you again?"

"Look for me in the bright dance of the waves. In the foam upon the shore. Where you go, there, too, my heart goes."

Uncaring of the pain—what was one more stab when her soul was shattering?—she hooked her fingers beneath one of the scales of her newfound tail and ripped it free. Even as a dark current swirled in to bear her away to the Sea Witch, she flung the scale to shore.

The last thing she heard was the sobbing of her husband, the thin wail of their child.

∼

"OH, SUCH BOUNTY," crooned the Sea Witch as she captured Muireen's tears. "Not only mourning the loss of your love but of your baby. Such power."

At last Muireen pulled away from the witch, shuddering, her grief drained dry.

"A pity that's the last of it." The Sea Witch held up the vial containing Muireen's sorrow. "Or is it? Tell me—where is your missing scale?" She pointed at the gap in Muireen's tail.

"I threw it to him," Muireen said, defiantly.

"Ahh. Listen then, and I will offer you joy and despair in equal measure. Every year, upon this anniversary, I can use my magic to let you see the world of the mortals, via the scale you left behind. I hope your husband keeps it safe and close by."

"He will."

"Then you will be able to gaze upon him, and your child, for a brief time And when you say farewell and once again the anguish falls upon you, I will take it for my own uses. Do you agree?"

"Will he be able to see me, too?"

"Of course, for that will make the pain all the greater." The witch gave her a horrible smile. "Since your pain prolongs my life, I welcome it."

Muireen did not like to think she was helping the Sea Witch in any way. And yet, to be able to see Eiric and her daughter once a year, however briefly, was a chance she could not refuse.

"Very well."

"Good! And luckily you'll be out of the palace dungeons next year, just in time. Now go, back to your foolish father and worthless siblings, and give them my regards."

Again the dark current bore Muireen through the reaches of the sea, depositing her where the indigo water faded into greeny blue. Tiredly, she swam toward the pearly towers of the palace, ready to bear whatever punishment her father thought just.

Some day, though, she vowed she would make the Sea Witch reunite her and her mortal love.

THE FIRST TIME the silver scale lit with Muireen's image, Eiric thought he was dreaming. Gods knew, he dreamt of her constantly. But to his surprise, he could hear her, too.

"I have not much time, love," she said. "It is only through

the magic of the Sea Witch that I may look upon you. Tell me, how do you fare? And our child?"

He showed her Brea, sleeping in her crib, told her all was well. Too soon, the light of the scale began to dim.

"When shall I see you again?" he cried.

"Next year." Her voice faded, and the cool silvery blue scale reflected back the light of his candle.

Ah, the pain was worse after seeing her face. And yet, knowing that she still lived, that she cared for him and their child, was enough to soothe the worst of the ache.

Every year, for a brief time, magic imbued the scale and Eiric was able to tell Muireann he loved her still. For he did, the flame of that love still burning fresh within him. He showed her how their daughter grew, and shared her milestones—first steps, first words, first swim in the sea which, thankfully, had not resulted in her sprouting fins or a tail.

"She is not a mer," Muireann said, "for never have our kind bred true with humans."

"I'm not certain she's entirely human, though," Eiric replied. "There is an odd touch of magic about her."

"Then perhaps she's a fey water creature of some kind. But she must find her own destiny."

Then the scale went quiet, and all other words must wait for another year.

It was not a pleasant thing, to bide so long, but it was enough. Eiric replayed their brief conversations in his head, traced her beloved features in memory, over and over. Their daughter grew into a lonely, quiet girl, and his heart ached within him for her solitude. He never spoke of her mother. That burden he would bear alone.

MANY YEARS PASSED, until one day while Eiric was out on his boat, the sky darkened with a sudden storm. He'd weathered storms aplenty but this one felt different—full of menace. He quickly stowed his nets, the memory of the fierce gale that had nearly taken his life shivering through him.

This storm tasted the same, the air heavy and metallic with the rising wind.

Then it was upon him, waves churning, spray blinding his eyes. This time, he was too far from land, fishing over the deep waters. There would be no escape from the ocean's wrath.

Still, he tried, fighting to keep his boat upon the waves and not under them, bailing when he could. Although Brea was nearly grown, he did not want to leave her an orphan, both parents lost to the sea.

But he was given no choice in the matter. A great, black wave rose over his boat, then smashed down, punching him to the depths.

Eiric floated, blinking against the salt water burning his eyes. Here, beneath the waves, it was strangely peaceful. The last of his breath left his body in a silver strand of bubbles, racing away toward the roiling surface. He let them go.

Then Muireann was there, floating before him. She pressed a bottle to his lips and he drank, then gagged on the foul secretion.

"Swallow it," she said, tears in her voice. "I cannot you save you, otherwise."

Coldness all about him, Eiric swallowed. Then screamed

as the cold burned away. Something terrible was happening to him, yet his sea maiden held him close.

Finally, shuddering, the pain passed. He looked up at his beloved.

"Are we dead?" he asked, amazed to find he could form the words.

"No, my love." She smiled at him. "You are no longer human, however. There is no return to the surface for you."

"As long as I might remain here, beneath the sea with you, I care not. Wherever you go—"

"There my heart also goes," she finished the words for him.

Together, webbed hands clasped, they swam, tails flashing through the water. Away from the storm and darkness, away from the cold, to an enchanted palace in the far south, made of shining coral.

There they rule to this day, wearing crowns of pearl and mantles of kelp, the Sea Queen and her once-mortal love.

AUTHOR'S NOTE: The story first appeared in Once Upon A Kiss, an anthology of romantic faerietale retellings. *The Little Mermaid* was my inspiration for this story. And while I wanted to incorporate some of the tragic elements from Hans Christian Andersen's original tale, I still wanted a fairytale happy ending for Muireen and her fisherman, no matter the sorrow it took them to get there.

FAERIE SONG

THE MUSIC CAME DRIFTING every black of the moon, winding like smoke through the dank alleyways of Hamelin's old town. *Come*, it whispered, the haunting melody compelling the vermin of the streets. *Come away.*

They did: the skittering roaches, the fluttering moths whose grubs ruined stored grain, the rats who infested the slums.

And the children.

Orphans, mostly, and those cast out, unwanted, one too many mouths to feed—or caught pilfering, and given the choice of the crowded prison or the call of the street.

Nobody knew precisely what happened to them, after.

Just that they were gone, those pests that caused trouble for the already strained resources of Hamelin. Better not to look too closely at the walled stronghold of the Strigosa Conservatory, whose magic kept the city clean.

Only those children trapped behind the walls knew what fate awaited. For most, it was a short life of hard drudgery. Those girls and boys fortunate enough to be graced with fair faces were quietly sent to serve in the houses of the barons and magistrates of the city. The less-pretty children were set to work in the conservatory, either toiling without pay in the workshops or tending to the everyday needs of the Pipers and their students.

For students there were—lucky, or unlucky, depending on who was doing the asking.

Every child pulled through the imposing gates of the Strigosa Conservatory was tested for musical ability. Those that showed aptitude were assigned to one of the Pipers, those forbidding men and women that guarded the secret of the Calling. It was not an easy apprenticeship, no matter what the servant children thought. The Pipers meted out harsh discipline for any infraction. Whether a student misbehaved or simply missed a note, the punishment was the same.

Linnet Sheeran leaned forward from her vantage point atop the roof of the dining hall and winced as the coarse cloth of her robe scraped the welts on her back. That afternoon, she had botched the fingering on a difficult passage of notes, and suffered five lashings as a result.

The beating was supposed to keep her meek and obedient, and in the past it had done so.

But not tonight.

Maybe it was the restless energy of the Calling, or the hot autumn wind that bore the smell of smoke and despair.

The poorest quarter of Hamelin had burned two days ago, and the Pipers were expecting a handful of children at the gates. Barbed curiosity had brought Linnet to the small stair leading to the roof. Those students who knew of the twisty staircase half-concealed at the back of the upper linen closet guarded their secret closely. The roof was the only refuge they had. They never spoke of it, and if another orphan had claimed the roof, the protocol was to retreat until the first student left.

That night, the rooftop was deserted, and Linnet pressed herself into the shelter of one of the tall chimneys. The music of the Calling swirled coaxingly around her.

Stop, she told it. *I am already here.*

The woven strands of notes paid her no heed. She was thankful that it was easier to ignore that aching summons from inside the walls of the conservatory.

Pipes—clear and high—played the melody, supported by violins, lutes, and the heartbeat throb of skin-covered drums. It was a lullaby and lament, a promise and a lie, and despite herself, Linnet swayed to that beat.

She winced as her robe pulled across her abraded back again. Clenching her teeth, she willed herself to stillness and watched the wide courtyard. Cloisters enclosed the plaza on three sides. In those shadowed corridors, flickering lamps revealed the hooded figures of the musicians at their work.

They faced the fortified wall that blocked the conservatory from the rest of the world. There was no egress or entry except through the iron doors and barbed portcullis, which were kept tightly locked and guarded.

Except on nights of the Calling, when the Pipers' magic ensured there could be no escape. Any creature venturing through those forbidding doors was going one direction only: straight into the clutches of the Strigosa Conservatory.

The gates were thrown open, and already the first trickle of vermin was entering. The air blurred with moth wings, and the darting shapes of bats who had come for the summoned feast. The ground shifted as roaches and rats skittered in from the city.

As the music reached a crescendo, the tide swelled. The hooded shapes of the Pipers emerged from the arches surrounding the courtyard. A pair of violinists moved to the right, playing a variation on the melody, and the slick brown mass of roaches veered to follow.

The music led them in a headlong rush over the edge of a metal vat filled with lamp oil, the sides slick and curved inward. When the last insects plummeted inside, the vat would be torched. The stink of that burning would linger in the courtyard for days.

On the other side of the courtyard, a group of pipe players coaxed the rats into a narrow gutter that led down beneath the conservatory. Linnet wasn't exactly certain what fate awaited them there, but none of the rodents ever emerged again.

One melody remained, supported by lutes and the thud of drums, and this was the hardest of all to ignore. Linnet kept her breathing slow, fighting the urge to slide recklessly down the roofs into the courtyard two stories below and prostrate herself at the feet of the single figure standing in the center.

The Master Piper.

None of the students knew who it was. Linnet suspected most of the instructors were equally ignorant. The Master Piper never spoke, merely communicated with music and gesture, and written missives when needed.

The Master might be stern Piper Michael, or quiet-voiced Piper Amalia. They might be young, or old, foreign or born in Hamelin itself. It didn't matter.

All that mattered was that they alone wielded the power to call the children.

Two came, holding hands, their faces smudged with ashes, clothing torn and blackened. A sister and brother, Linnet guessed, survivors of the recent fires. It seemed the rest of their family had not been so lucky.

Eyes wide with terror and wonder, they crept beneath the sharp portcullis and past the black iron doors.

Go back! Linnet wanted to shout at them. *Before it's too late!*

But it was already too late.

The only escape now would be if some relative or kindly patron appeared to claim them before the next Calling. Meantime, they would be washed and fed and tested for musical aptitude, but no determination of their fate would be made for another month.

Then, if no one had come to rescue the unfortunate orphans, they would be put to use however the conservatory pleased.

And, most likely, broken apart.

The pain of losing her little sister ripped through Linnet, and she bent her face to her knees to muffle her sob.

"Watch after Tallia," Mama had croaked—the last words she'd spoken before death crept, cold and gray, over her body.

Not even the hot tears of her daughters had been able to wake her. Sobbing, Linnet had bade her sister to turn away, then dragged Mama's body to lie beside Papa's for the collectors to gather up on the morrow.

"I promise," she whispered fiercely to her mother's unseeing face. "I will care for Tallia, no matter what."

There was a little bread and grain left, and their rooms,

though filled with the lingering stench of sickness, would give them enough shelter.

The next day, she'd gone out begging and garnered enough coppers to keep them fed for a time on spoiled fruit and cheese rinds. At least water from the public fountains was free, despite its metallic taste. They might not thrive, but they would survive.

And then the dark of the moon had come, and with it, the Calling.

Linnet flinched from the memory—more painful than the welts on her back—and squinted at the new arrivals.

The children were too far away for her to tell if they were pretty enough to be house servants. That was the best fate, she thought. Even if the servants were treated poorly, at least they would be out from under the crushing grip of the conservatory.

That would have been her fate. Both she and Tallia were winsome enough, underneath the dirt and grime; at least, that's what the matron said who had given them their first rough scrubbing when they arrived.

"Bound for the houses," the woman had muttered.

"Will they separate us?" Linnet had asked, her voice thin with fear.

"Mayhap," the matron had answered, uncaring of their fate. "Though some of the nobles like a matched pair."

Linnet had clung to that hope, along with Tallia's small, moist hand, until the Pipers had separated them for testing.

The Pipers had murmured together when she sang back the notes played to her, nodded as she clapped in time to the drums. At the end of the testing, though, she was only able to produce a grotesque squawking noise on the pipe. Tears rising hotly in her eyes, she'd tried, over and over. But the mouthpiece felt strange against her lips, the vibrating reed inert unless she blew mightily, with horrible result.

"Not suited," Piper Michael had said, shaking his head as he took the instrument from her.

"Wait!" she had cried, reaching for the bell-flared wooden pipe. "Let me try again... please."

Surely Tallia had the same musical abilities. They were sisters, after all, and Linnet had vowed to care for her, no matter what. She could not fail at this. She must not abandon Tallia to face the conservatory alone.

"You have attempted it enough." The Piper's voice was as cold as the flagstones beneath her feet.

He pulled the pipe out of reach and then gestured to one of the other Pipers standing in a solemn row in the stone-walled testing room. Each of them held an instrument, in descending order of importance: violin, lute, drum.

The Piper who stepped forward had a sweet face, but her eyes were hard.

"Hold out your left arm," she said in a voice as quiet as mist.

Linnet complied, and the Piper set the violin on Linnet's shoulder, guided her hand to rest around the instrument's neck. After a few adjustments, the Piper handed Linnet the bow, demonstrating how to fold her fingers over the slender wooden stick.

"Now, place the bow on the string and try to produce a sound," the Piper said. The flatness in her voice suggested she expected Linnet to fail at this instrument, too.

Biting her lip in concentration, Linnet set the white hair of the bow to the silvery strings. She drew in a deep breath, and then pulled her arm back. At first only a dry creaking sound emitted.

Before the Piper could take the instrument from her, Linnet moved her right arm faster. The creak turned to a note. Wobbly and uncertain, but still—a note.

"Hm." The Piper nodded at the violin. "Play the next string."

Pursing her mouth with effort, Linnet shot a glance at the strings, and noticed she had tilted the end of the instrument higher than the Piper had shown her. She corrected, then carefully moved the bow to the indicated string.

This time, she began the bow stroke more quickly. The initial groaning note smoothed out almost immediately into a tone that, if not quite pleasant, was at least not horrendous.

Expression blank, the Piper directed her to the next string, and the next. Each time, Linnet was able to produce a stronger sound, and her heart fluttered with hope.

"That will do," the Piper said, taking the violin from the cradle of Linnet's shoulder and plucking the bow from her hand. "I am Piper Amalia. From now on, you will be my student."

Grim-faced Piper Michael gave a single, short nod, and the matter was settled.

Buoyant with hope, Linnet returned to the dormitory–to discover that Tallia had failed every musical test. Her sister would be sent to serve in some noble's house. Alone.

Regret had pierced Linnet's heart, a jagged sword, twisting and twisting. If only she had known! If only she had accepted her failure on the pipes, instead of fighting so hard to prove herself. She'd been stupid, and had not thought to hide her talent. Though how was she to know that Tallia didn't have the same abilities?

Linnet had wept, had begged, had even tried to break her fingers in the door so that she would be too crippled to play. The Pipers had only put her in the infirmary under strict watch, cutting short her remaining time with her sister.

"It will be all right," Linnet had said at their last meeting, trying to keep the tears from coursing down her cheeks. She gave her sister a tight hug, her left hand clumsy with bandages. "I'll come for you, I swear it."

Wide-eyed, Tallia nodded. Her thin face was pale, her eyes desolate as the matron had pulled her away.

"Lin!" she'd cried, stretching her arms out.

"Be strong," Linnet had called after her. "Watch for me. I love you!"

Then she'd laid her head back on the hard pillow and wept until her body was a hollow husk of grief.

That had been three years ago.

At first, she'd plotted to run away, but it was impossible. Then she'd tried to "lose" her musical ability, pretending she could not produce any pleasing tone on the violin or keep to a solid rhythm.

That result had been a beating so severe she could scarcely walk for several weeks. Once she'd recovered, Piper Amalia had given her a choice.

"Either apply yourself, or serve in the midden. I needn't remind you it's ugly work."

Shoveling the conservatory's waste was, indeed, among the worst jobs. Linnet had quashed her rebellion and agreed to focus her efforts on the violin once more.

She held to the slim hope that, somehow, learning the

magic behind the Piper's music would enable her to escape and find Tallia.

I'm sorry. The refrain threaded through her every heartbeat. *I'm trying to come, Tallia. Hold fast.*

There was no news of her sister. No gossip of the outside world passed the high, forbidding walls of the conservatory. But she had to believe that Tallia was well, and waiting for her somewhere out there in Hamelin.

The force of her promise kept Linnet moving forward, even when she wanted to give up in despair. Piper Amalia was a harsh taskmaster, as all Pipers were, with little patience for the stumbles of a beginner. No matter how hard Linnet practiced, it was never enough.

"Barely adequate," the Piper often declared at the end of their grueling two-hour sessions. "Perhaps the drum would be a better fit for you."

"I'll work harder," Linnet always said, throat tight with frustration and fear.

"See that you do."

Piper Amalia never spoke a word of praise. Even when Linnet mastered a new aspect of the violin, the Piper would just set her another task. Basic scales turned to dizzying arpeggios in triple-time, simple note-reading developed into the expectation that Linnet would be able to glance at a page of music and immediately play the composition without error.

Thrice a week Linnet endured her lessons. Even if she were unwell, she was expected to drag herself from the sickbed. One did not miss a session with a Piper unless it was physically impossible to play.

The other students had it no better. A quiet current of

grim commiseration ran through the dormitory, but no one spoke of their misery openly. Just last year, one of the older students had complained a bit too vigorously. The next morning they were gone, along with their clothing and few possessions.

No explanation was given, and the students, after exchanging quick, horrified glances, never spoke of that particular individual again.

There were more than a dozen of them, boys on one side of the wall, girls on the other. Everyone wore homespun brown robes, with the black badge of the Pipers sewn on the right-hand side to denote their status as apprentices of music.

Despite the harsh environment, Linnet found solace in playing. And she clung to the hope that, somehow, music would be the key to her freedom. She grew taller over the years, and finally the Pipers judged her grown enough to move to a full-sized instrument.

The new violin was a rich chestnut color, with a deep, sweet tone. When Linnet stroked the bow across the strings, the instrument sang back to her, the vibration of each note resonating through her jaw and collarbone.

It was dangerous to care for anything inside the cold walls of the conservatory, but she fell desperately in love with the curved wood, the shining strings. She practiced constantly, and was rewarded at her next lesson.

"Hmph," Piper Amalia said, her inflection rising with the barest hint of approval. "I suppose we shall begin teaching you the first refrain of the Calling."

Linnet swallowed back her leap of anticipation and meekly bowed her head. "If you see fit, Piper."

Inside, her heart thumped with excitement. At last, the

magical secrets of the conservatory would begin to open for her. And maybe, just maybe, there was a way she could use that knowledge to escape.

Piper Amalia narrowed her eyes, as if sensing Linnet's thoughts. "Do not expect to participate in the summons until you have memorized every phrase necessary. The notes may seem simple, but harnessing their power can take months. Years, even."

"I understand."

"Do you?" Her teacher regarded her coldly. "You are not allowed to remove the sheet music from my sight. You must remember what I have played here today, and practice the notes exactly as I have demonstrated."

Linnet nodded. Privately, she vowed to master the first refrains as quickly as possible. Those students who did so were moved from the dormitory to a room of their own, with less supervision than the other apprentices. That was the first step to gaining her freedom.

"You must not play the phrase *anywhere* but in the practice rooms reserved for the Calling music," her teacher said, setting a sheet of parchment on the music stand. "Do you agree to do so?"

"Yes, Piper. Of course."

"Breaking this rule is punishable by death." Piper Amalia gave her a grimace that was probably supposed to pass for a smile. "That is, if you survive the consequences of disobeying."

A chill ran down Linnet's spine, dousing her excitement.

There were stories, of course, whispered tales of students hideously devoured by the results of their Calling practice. Whether eaten alive by rats or irrevocably twisted by magic gone awry, none could say for certain.

Only that, even within the shielded rooms the Pipers set aside for such perilous practice, terrible things might happen.

Outside of those magically protected spaces, it was guaranteed.

"Follow along," Piper Amalia said, nodding to the sheet of music on the stand. "I will play the first sequence."

Subdued, Linnet focused her attention on the music. Only half the page was inscribed with notes. The Pipers safeguarded their secrets, and she wondered if there were any pages containing the entire score of the Calling.

Probably not.

Her teacher began to play. First a low throbbing tone, then a sweeping run upward. Even though it was a fragment of secondary melody, the music caught something inside Linnet. She took an involuntary step forward, nearly toppling the music stand.

Piper Amalia stopped, frowning. "You must harden yourself, or you will play your own heart out into the open—which is a gruesome sight, I assure you."

Pressing her lips together, Linnet shuffled back to her place.

"How do I prevent such a thing?" she asked, her throat dry with apprehension.

"Forget. Sever your longings. You are but a vessel for the music to pour through." Piper Amalia narrowed her eyes. "Perhaps you are still too young."

Linnet's breath constricted. "I'm not, I promise. I'll do as you say."

It was the only chance she had.

Though she could not imagine setting aside the hot, yearning grief she carried just beneath her heart—even if she wanted to. The memory of her promise to Tallia was the only thing she had left of her sister. Of her entire family.

A cold wind swept across the rooftop, pulling Linnet from her thoughts. Below, the music of the newest Calling ebbed, and the two fresh orphans stumbled away with one of the matrons. For their sakes, Linnet hoped someone would come to claim them.

The shadowed quiet of the courtyard was broken by the rattle of the portcullis descending, the ponderous creak of the metal doors swinging shut until they closed with a hollow clang. They would not open again for another month.

There was, however, a small tunnel through the walls for the Pipers to use between Callings. It was enclosed by two smaller doors and continuously guarded by the grim soldiers who served the conservatory. Rumors held that the passage was also protected with dire magic. Unless one knew the proper sequence of notes to sing, the enchantment would slice the hapless traveler clean across the throat.

Linnet didn't doubt it.

She'd heard the whispers that one of the conservatory's suppliers, overeager to make his delivery and be gone, had stepped into the corridor too soon. It had taken three servant orphans a full day to scrub the walls clean of his blood.

With a shiver, she waited in the shelter of the chimney for the last Pipers to clear the courtyard, so that she might sneak back to the dormitory. The night had turned chilly, but the Master Piper still stood facing the gates. Two other Pipers silently moved to stand beside him.

"A pity we did not gather more children," one of them said.

Some trick of the acoustics brought their conversation drifting up to the roof. Linnet held her breath and leaned forward. The Pipers never spoke together where students might hear.

The Master Piper gave a long, slow nod.

"Do you think…" the second Piper glanced over her shoulder, then turned back to the Master. "Did *they* steal our harvest?"

They? Who could the Piper be speaking of? Linnet could not imagine anyone daring to oppose the power of the Strigosa Conservatory.

The Master Piper made no response, and the first Piper shook his head.

"They would not be so bold, nor is their magic strong enough. Compared to our might, their foolish little tunes are nothing. We have nothing to fear from the fae—even if they are rumored to have infiltrated the forest."

Linnet caught her breath, her heart squeezing with hope. The fae truly existed? And they had music magic?

"Still," the female Piper said, "you must be aware of the stories. They once were powerful."

"Folktales, embellished over the years," the first Piper began, but was cut off by the Master raising an abrupt hand.

Slowly, that central figure turned, hooded face upturned to the rooftops.

Ice running down her spine, Linnet shrank back against the rough brickwork of the chimney and closed her eyes, praying the Piper would not sense her. She breathed shallowly through her nose, slowly counting. Until she reached one hundred, she wouldn't dare stir from her hiding place.

Even when she heard the Pipers' footsteps receding over the flagstones, she remained still and quiet. Her leg cramped, but she gritted her teeth and ignored it.

At the count of eighty-seven, a final set of footsteps echoed across the courtyard, growing fainter within the cloisters until the sound was cut off by the thud of a door closing.

Panicked realization squeezed a single, hot tear from Linnet's eye. It trailed, cooling, down her cheek. Whoever had remained would have caught her, if she hadn't set herself to the utmost caution.

She didn't know what the punishment was for eavesdropping on the Pipers, but she doubted she would have survived it.

It took a long time for her to calm her frantic pulse. The courtyard appeared deserted, but she shuddered, imagining eyes watching her from the dark arches of the cloisters. Finally, she gathered enough courage to creep out from behind the shelter of the chimney and traverse the exposed slate shingles. She wasn't able to take a full breath until she'd reached the dormitory without mishap.

Still trembling, she slipped under the scratchy woolen blanket of her thin pallet. Sleep was impossible, of course, with the aftermath of her fear still racing through her. The Pipers' words echoed in her mind. *Faeries. In the forest.*

If it were true—and it must be, otherwise why would the Pipers speak of such things?—then the fae folk had come to the Buchewald, the dense wooded expanse outside of Hamelin.

Why? Could they help her? And even if they would, how could she reach them?

There were no answers. Finally her tangled thoughts unknotted enough for her to sleep, though it was a restless, uneasy night.

Linnet woke the next morning feeling singed around the

edges, as though she were a piece of parchment that had lain too close to the flame. At least she would not have to face Piper Amalia that day.

And, she remembered with a jolt, she had permission to use a shielded practice room.

As the other students rose and dressed, obeying the summons of the morning bell, she closed her eyes. Blocking out the sound of their voices, she closed her eyes and recalled the phrase that Piper Amalia had played for her the day before. At the very end of their lengthy lesson, the teacher had finally allowed Linnet to attempt the notes on her violin.

Only when she'd played the phrase perfectly a dozen times in a row had the Piper decreed she was ready to practice it on her own.

"It is not just the notes, you understand," Piper Amalia had said, "but channeling their power. *That* is what you must learn to do, without letting it turn on you."

Those dire words ringing in her ears, Linnet got up, donned her homespun robe, and ate the usual bowl of watery gruel served for breakfast. After that, there was nothing else to do but gather her violin and go to the shielded practice rooms.

It wasn't quite that simple, of course.

Even though she was permitted to be there, Linnet's heart pounded as she approached the wide desk nearly spanning the corridor leading to the rooms. A Piper sat there, a sheaf of papers at his elbow, and a bored-looking guard stood sentinel.

"Name?" the Piper asked when Linnet halted before the desk.

"Linnet Sheeran." Her voice was scratchy in her throat.

The Piper pulled his stack of papers over and ran his finger down the list of names inscribed on the first page.

"Room three is currently open," he said, then gestured at the iron-bound clock squatting on the corner of the desk. "You have two hours allotted daily."

"I won't exceed them," she promised, wondering at the note of warning in his voice.

He looked up, an arid spark of humor in his brown eyes. "There's little chance of that. I presume this is your first practice session?"

She nodded.

"Well then." He motioned for her to proceed past him. "Second door on the left. Good luck."

Without waiting for a reply, he turned back to his papers.

Linnet pressed her lips together and stepped around the edge of the desk. No sound escaped from the doors on either side as she passed. She paused a moment before the room the Piper had indicated, then turned the plain brass handle and stepped inside.

Unlike the other practice rooms in the conservatory, this one held no music stand. The walls and floor were paneled in pale birch wood, and there was enough space that even with her arms stretched wide, she wouldn't be able to touch the walls on either side. A diffuse light came from the ceiling, the same silver glow that illuminated the Pipers' areas of the complex.

Students and drudges made do with smoky lanterns and weak candle flames, and her breath hitched with excitement at this proof that her station was improving.

She set her violin case on the low bench running along one side of the small room, then carefully unpacked her instrument. It gleamed in the light, the wood shining with subtle reflections, the strings picking out glints of silver.

Curious how the magical shielding would affect the sound of her violin, she set the bow on the strings. Simple scales first, to limber up her fingers and bow arm.

To her surprise, the notes sounded warm and unmuffled —clearer than if she were playing in a normal practice room, stronger than in Piper Amalia's somewhat cluttered rooms. Smiling, Linnet leaned into the sound, experimenting with speed and pressure as she stroked her bow across the strings.

The instrument vibrated under her chin, as though happy to be awake.

Once she was sufficiently warmed up, she paused to replay the Calling's counter-melody in her mind. *Start on the lowest string; a long, mournful tone followed by a flurry of notes sweeping higher, like a gust of wind rounding up stray leaves. Then linger, high and yearning, like a lost piece of a lullaby...*

When she was certain she had the phrase firmly fixed in her head, she lifted her violin and began.

At first, they were simply notes—just as when she'd played them during her lesson. *Channel their power*, Piper Amalia had said. But how?

Closing her eyes as she played, Linnet tried to recall the pulling sensation she'd felt on the roof, as the Pipers performed the Calling in the courtyard below. A tug, a twist deep in the gut... yes, there it was!

A wave of nausea washed over her and she stopped abruptly, trying to hold back her breakfast. With shaking hands, she set her violin in its case, then gulped air, battling back the roiling in her belly.

So. Either she'd had a bad bowl of porridge or—more likely—had managed to touch the power of the Calling.

But how was she to practice the phrase when doing so meant running the risk of becoming violently ill? The Piper at the desk's grim amusement suddenly made sense—as did the general disposition of the Pipers in general. If harnessing the magic meant a constant battle to keep one's internal organs behaving, no wonder they were such a sour and forbidding lot.

Maybe she didn't after all, want to control the music magic.

Far too late for that, however.

After several minutes, she felt sufficiently recovered to try again. Surely there was a point where she could touch the power of the Calling without her body rebelling. The Pipers clearly did it all the time.

It took several more brushes with nausea, and one point when it felt her heart would burst out of her chest, but Linnet was finally able to play the beginning of the phrase. There was a point halfway through the ascending run, however, where she lost control of the power every time.

Sweating and shaking, she continued attempting the notes, but each time was worse than the one before. If she kept trying, she was in serious danger of collapsing, or dropping her instrument, or both. Neither of which were acceptable, in the eyes of the Pipers.

Defeated, she packed up her instrument and left the room.

The hallway was as quiet as before. When she walked by the desk, the Piper glanced at the clock.

"Forty-three minutes," he said. "Surprisingly good for a first try."

Exhausted, Linnet managed a nod. She needed to bathe, and then, once her stomach settled, drink some tea, and probably take a rest. Forty-three minutes! She couldn't imagine how she'd feel after two hours of struggling to master the Calling.

She slept through lunch, which was not a bad thing, as her stomach still protested at dinner. Still, she managed to get some sustenance in, and didn't bother fighting the weariness that rolled in afterward.

Sometime in the dark of the night, she jolted awake, a strange melody weaving through the air. Quieting her breathing, Linnet listened, but only the snores of the sleeping students reached her ears.

Had she imagined the sound? It had seemed so clear, so true—the sweet lilting of pipes, like nothing she'd ever heard before. The melody had reminded her of the Calling somehow, but warmer, less demanding. Under her breath, Linnet tried to hum the already-fading tune, but only managed to hold onto a snippet of melody.

In the morning, the ethereal tune had faded. The lingering echoes evaporated, washed away by the rising tide of the day and the forbidding prospect of facing the Calling once again.

This time, Linnet skipped breakfast altogether. It would be easier to fight nausea if she had nothing in her belly. The same Piper granted her access to the shielded practice area, this time assigning her to room four.

It looked exactly the same as room three, except that the door was on the opposite side. Linnet unpacked her violin, warmed up, and, with a deep breath, tackled the counter-melody of the Calling.

It was easier to balance the pull of the music this time, and she managed to reach the upper notes twice before her body was overtaken by a fit of shaking. After that, she made little progress, and had to admit defeat.

"Twenty-seven minutes," the Piper at the desk pronounced as she passed. "Disappointing."

She did not look at him, but scurried away down the corridor, head bowed. No doubt Piper Amalia would say the same at her lesson that afternoon.

Indeed, her teacher was more harsh than usual. But at the end of the lesson, to Linnet's surprise, Piper Amalia gave her another phrase of the Calling to learn.

"Piper Heinrich reports that you are making satisfactory progress," the teacher said. "Many students new to the Calling cannot bear to practice for more than ten minutes at a time. Now, listen."

Linnet did, committing the new phrases to memory, though her heart sank at the thought of the trials to come. What would these next notes do—give her blinding headaches? Make the blood constrict in her veins until she could no longer bear her own weight?

Whatever the music might do, however, refusing to play it was not an option.

At least she was able to consume a hearty lunch and dinner. Enough, she hoped, that it might sustain her through the morrow's practice session.

That night, a haunting melody pulled her from sleep once more. This time, she hummed it right away, determined to commit the notes to memory.

In the quiet dawn light, as she slipped from dreaming to wakefulness, she heard it again. This time, a fragment of the tune remained lodged in her mind. She was careful not to hum it where anyone might hear.

The only music allowed in the Strigosa Conservatory was assigned by the Pipers. Once, Linnet had overheard another student playing a half-remembered lullaby. Apparently, the Pipers had heard him, too, for the boy was in the infirmary for months afterward.

In the practice room—back to number three this time—Linnet dared to play the half-remembered notes before beginning her Calling practice. The tune began on the D, went up a fourth, then, with a flicker of fingers, descended. Up again, one note higher, echo down, then leap the octave.

As she played, a sweet, golden warmth stole through her, as soothing as though her blood had turned to honey. Yearning for more, she tried to follow the melody into the next phrase, but her fingers stumbled and she lost the thread.

She halted, lifting her bow. Had she truly felt the power of the music, or was she imagining things? And if it was not her imagination, what would the Pipers do if they found out?

Suddenly cold, Linnet stopped chasing the sweet song and turned her focus back to her true task: mastering the violin part of the Calling.

Perhaps it was the steadying effect of the elusive melody, but she was able to finish playing the first phrase of music Piper Amalia had given her without collapsing. Swallowing back nausea, she took a short break, then started on the new part.

The phrase—a jagged minor arpeggio—felt like ice stabbing through her lungs. Gasping, she tried to push through, but each note was more painful than the last.

Finally, sobbing, she stopped.

The neck of her violin felt like a thick block between her chilled fingers, the bow nothing more than a clumsy length of wood and horsehair.

Unbidden, the night melody sounded again in her mind. Before she could think too deeply, she began to play. Unlike the notes of the Calling, the sweet, simple phrase unfurled like sunshine. She played it three times through, until her breath flowed calm and her fingers warmed and steadied on the notes.

Magic.

And not any kind known to the conservatory, of that she was strangely certain. There was only one other place she could think of where it might be coming from: the fae.

Somehow, for reasons she could not fathom, faeries were singing to her in her sleep. But why? What could one apprentice violinist do with a faerie song, against the combined might of the Pipers and their Calling?

Mulling over the unanswerable question, she packed up and left the practice room. The Piper at the desk—Piper Heinrich, she presumed—gave her a sharp look as she passed.

"One hour," he said, a note of surprise in his voice.

Too late, she remembered to bow her shoulders and drag her steps, to feign the effects of battling the Calling for a solid hour. She thought of telling him she had practiced something else instead; one of her concertos, or nothing except scales, but that would certainly lead to a beating.

So she held her tongue and slouched away down the hall, mentally berating her own foolishness.

The Pipers must not discover the fae music—especially not if it had the power to nullify the effects of their own dire magic.

Over the next few weeks, Linnet fell into a strange rhythm. At night, she dreamed and woke and tried to grasp the strands of faerie song. By day, she worked to master the Calling, driven by an urgency she did not understand.

She did not repeat her earlier mistake, however, of emerging unscathed from the practice room. It was easy enough to end with the newest phrase from Piper Amalia, which invariably left her shaking and sick.

"Tomorrow night is the Calling," her teacher announced at the end of her next lesson. "You have been granted permission to attend."

Linnet paused in packing up her violin and blinked at the Piper. "I have?"

Either this was excellent news, or the Pipers were planning to unmask her somehow, denounce her for playing illicit music and throw her out of the conservatory. Or worse.

"Yes." Piper Amalia folded her hands primly at her waist. "You have made such good progress—due in large part to my teaching, of course—that you've been deemed ready to observe the performance of our most solemn duty."

Linnet was supposed to watch then, and not play. Understandable, considering she'd not yet learned the entire countermelody. Although she suspected she was getting close.

Piper Amalia's teaching had little to do with it, however. The steadying effect of the faerie song was the only thing that enabled Linnet to move through the various phrases of the Calling so quickly without horrible suffering.

"Thank you, Piper," she said, in what she hoped was a reverent tone as she finished packing away her violin. She must give no sign that she had, in fact, seen the Calling before.

"In addition," her teacher said, "you are to be given your own room, immediately."

Linnet bowed her head. "I'm most grateful."

This time, she meant every word.

Her own space, at last! She wouldn't have to worry about her faerie-filled dreams, or that her soft humming of forbidden melodies might wake the students slumbering on either side.

"As you should be. You may skip practice tomorrow, since close proximity to the Calling can be… taxing, and you will need all your strength. Come to the courtyard an hour before midnight. And wear this."

Piper Amalia handed her a hooded black robe. The material was a finer weave than Linnet's brown robes, the dark cloth smooth under her fingers.

"The violins will be gathered on the right," the Piper continued. "Stand behind us, out of the way. Say nothing. When the Calling is over, you may return to your room. Now, go. One of the servants will show you to your new quarters."

Linnet bobbed a curtsey, then took up her violin case in her free hand and left the Piper's study.

As promised, a servant was waiting outside. Sullenly, the girl led Linnet to the wing where the more advanced students lived. Linnet forced herself not to skip ahead with excitement. Soon, with the help of the faerie song, she might be able to win free of the Strigosa Conservatory, and finally rescue her sister. The thought glittered inside her, a jubilant counterpoint to the clammy, mold-scented hallway.

The servant halted at a door midway down the dim corridor.

"Here," she said, gesturing to the botanical shape carved into the wood. "Fern."

Linnet nodded, then glanced across the hall, to see an acorn inscribed on the opposite door. It was a clumsier system than simple numbers, but she supposed the Pipers had their reasons. Thanking the girl, she lifted the cold metal latch and stepped inside

The door bolted from the inside, which she found somewhat amazing. Students were not expected to have any privacy—but then, she seemed to be rapidly approaching the status of becoming a full Piper.

The knowledge made her shiver. Not that she would ever agree to join their ranks.

Compared to the dormitory, the cramped space allotted to her seemed a palace. A single bed was pushed against the far wall beneath a single, high window covered with an iron crossbar. The bed was made up with the usual scratchy blanket and thick sheets, though the pillow looked a bit plumper than the one on her old bed.

A small wooden dresser, the dark wood showing plenty of wear, stood by the head of the bed. When she pulled open the top drawer, Linnet found that her extra robes and undergarments had been brought over from her dormitory chest. She had no other personal belongings, except for her violin.

She tucked the instrument at the foot of the bed, then carefully hung the black robe on a hook beside the door.

Was attending the Calling some kind of final test? She had very little idea what becoming a full Piper entailed. Once students were moved from the dormitory, they seemed to disappear.

She'd thought it was simply because the Pipers, with the

exception of the teachers, kept entirely to themselves. But what if something darker awaited? No one knew all the secrets the conservatory held. Except for the Master Piper, who never spoke.

Glancing at the dark fabric hung beside the door, she couldn't help wondering: was her first official Calling to be her last?

A grim melancholy tried to take root in her heart—but she pushed it aside, instead softly humming the faerie song. Whatever dire fate the conservatory had in store, she'd fight it with everything in her power.

THAT NIGHT, when the fae music woke her, Linnet opened her eyes to discover her room filled with a soft golden light. She sat, her breath catching when she saw the source of that glow —the figure of a winged woman hovering at the end of her bed.

The woman wore a gown woven of cobwebs and dewdrops. She seemed taller than a human, the delicate filigreed crown atop her head almost brushing the ceiling, and her face was oddly narrow, with large eyes and a pointed chin. Wisps of her long, bright hair floated about her, and her translucent wings shone like shafts of sunlight through a dark forest.

"Are you… a faerie?" Linnet whispered.

"Indeed," the woman answered softly. "I am Queen of the Fae, and I have come to ask your aid."

Linnet clasped the rough blanket tightly between her fingers. "Am I dreaming?"

"No more than any mortal dreams, awake or asleep. Surely you have heard us singing to you."

"I have." Linnet swallowed, moistening her dry throat. "But how can I possibly help you?"

The queen's eyes narrowed, and the brightness surrounding her sharpened like broken glass. "Tomorrow, you will be witness to a terrible magic. I and my people are coming to stop it, but we fear that such corrupt power is stronger than our own. Only with a human's aid might we prevail."

What did the faerie mean? Linnet felt as though she was expected to understand something just beyond her grasp.

"I'm not sure—" she began, but the queen suddenly whirled in agitation.

"Hush," she said. "We are nearly discovered."

Between one heartbeat and the next, she was gone, her brilliant light doused as though it had never been. Only the afterimage of her glowing figure remained, inscribed behind Linnet's eyelids.

She stayed sitting and wrapped her arms around her knees, trying to make sense of the Faerie Queen's visitation. The fae were coming to oppose the Calling, that much was clear, and expected Linnet to help them... somehow. The faerie song was the key, but she had no idea where the lock even was.

Soft footsteps sounded in the hallway outside, and through the crack under her door she saw a faint circle of light. It halted directly before her room.

Linnet held her breath and sat motionless, her heartbeat thundering in her chest. Who was there?

The latch rattled softly, and she squeezed her eyes closed,

as if doing so would make her invisible. The door was locked. Surely whoever was outside wouldn't be able to enter.

Finally, after what felt like a thousand hours, the person moved off and Linnet dared to open her eyes. The light grew fainter and fainter, until she was left alone in the darkness, her knees pulled tightly to her chest.

Slowly, muscles aching, she uncurled and lay down, pulling the cover up to her chin. Surely she would find no sleep that night.

To her surprise, though, she woke to a patch of sunlight on the floor, and the faerie song ringing through her head.

And the cold knowledge that at midnight the Calling would begin.

The day unfurled slowly, yet all too soon dusk fell. With it came the hushed anticipation that always filled the conservatory on Calling eve. In the courtyard, servants were pouring flammable oil into the roach cistern. Others prepared the lanterns within the cloisters. Linnet watched from a smudged window in the stairwell, her body tightening with fear.

What if the fae folk didn't come? What if they did, and were defeated by the Pipers? And what was her role in all this?

As bidden, she had not gone to the practice rooms that day. Instead, she'd taken out her violin in the privacy of her new room. Leaving the bow tucked inside her case, she had simply run the fingering of the faerie song over and over, making certain the melody was imprinted on her fingertips as surely as it was in her mind.

She planned to bring her instrument to the Calling, hidden beneath the voluminous folds of the black robe. As long as no one looked too closely—or bumped into her—she would be able to carry it undetected, if a bit awkwardly.

The Strigosa Conservatory quieted as the students and servants were sent to their beds. Linnet wondered if any of her former dormitory-mates would ascend to the roof that night. If so, she resolved not to look for them, for fear of giving their secret away.

The night was dark, and darker still as Linnet donned her robe and pulled the hood up over her head. She unpacked her violin and tucked it under her right elbow beneath the robe, adjusting the black fabric so it covered the instrument. The bow went in her other hand, the stick lying back along her arm and concealed by the robe's sleeve. It meant she couldn't bend her arm, but hopefully no one would notice.

With a deep breath, she left her room and joined the procession of Pipers making for the courtyard.

Luckily, everyone had their hoods drawn, and she was careful to lag near the back and keep to the shadows. It was simple enough to sidle around to the right when they reached the cloisters. She positioned herself to the side of the violinists, where the lump of her hidden instrument was partially obscured by her body. She hoped.

One of the Pipers turned to look at her, and Linnet stiffened. *Please, don't see the violin. Please.*

The figure gave her a single, sharp nod, and Linnet could just make out Piper Amalia's features beneath the hood. Then her teacher pivoted back to face the courtyard, and Linnet's heart resumed beating.

Almost imperceptibly, Pipers filled the spaces between the arches. The scattered lanterns picked out the flash of an eye here, the flared bole of a pipe there.

At some unseen signal, the drums began. They pulsed softly, the throbbing beat almost drowned out by the metal screech of the gates being pulled open, the clank of the portcullis raising.

Linnet craned, trying for a glimpse of the city beyond. From her spot deep in the cloistered hall, she could see very little: a wall-mounted torch, the shine of diamond-paned windows, the steep slope of a nearby roofline.

It was enough. The world outside existed, and soon she would go there—fates willing.

Fates, or the fae.

If the faeries won their battle, she might be free that very night! It was too exhilarating to contemplate, and she stuffed the dizzying thought away.

Lutes joined the drums, strumming a shifting series of diminished chords. The violinists stirred, bringing their instruments to their shoulders as a wedge of Pipers strode into the courtyard.

At their head was the Master Piper, hidden behind hood and robes. The other pipe players flanked that forbidding figure, and they halted as one, instruments at the ready.

The gates stood wide, the fanged portcullis fully raised. The Master raised one black-gloved hand, and the drums grew louder, the lutes more insistent. At the start of the next seven-count cycle, the pipes began, crying their melody into the night.

A measure later the violins joined them, playing the countermelody that Linnet had battled for most of the month. Hearing those notes—low, sweeping to high, then the serrated arpeggios—she staggered in place, sharp pains lancing through her stomach.

It was worse, a hundred times worse, than practicing the music on her own.

Hot tears squeezed from her eyes, and she gasped, trying to keep her violin and bow from slipping from her nerveless grasp. If she dropped them, they would shatter on the flagstones and all hope would be lost. For her, and for the fae.

She did not know how long she endured, sobbing quietly, biting the inside of her lip until she tasted blood.

The moths came. Then the roaches.

When half the violinists moved away to direct the insects, Linnet's pains eased slightly. She held back a groan and forced herself to straighten, using the wall for support while she focused on what was coming through the gates.

The rats, of course, skittering and wide-eyed with fear.

Then they, too, were led away, and there was a brief lull in the Calling—the calm before the torrent. She pulled in a shuddering breath, the momentary absence of pain a blessed relief.

The Master Piper stepped forward and began the poisonous melody that would gather all the lost children to come to Strigosa Conservatory. At the sound, Linnet's knees turned to water. Only the wall at her back kept her upright as the dreadful music poured forth.

Movement at the gates—a half dozen children, stumbling with weariness. And behind them…

Linnet froze, transfixed, as the fae folk passed between the gaping gates.

Strangely jointed creatures, creaking like wood as they moved. Dancing maidens with flowers in their hair, their skin so pale she could see the bones beneath. Small, sharp-toothed goblins, green-hued hags, a black horse with moonlit eyes.

Every creature from every tale she'd ever heard of, and more, poured in through the gates.

The drums faltered, and the lutes. The pipes fell away, until the only sound left was the playing of the Master Piper.

The fae folk halted just inside the walls, and Linnet could see the effect of the music on them. Some trembled like leaves before a storm. The maidens ceased dancing. The goblins cowered together.

A path cleared, and the golden, glowing Queen of the Fae glided through their midst, wings fluttering softly. Bright dust scattered behind her, and those it fell upon seemed to take heart, bravely following her as she landed directly in front of the Master Piper.

Slowly, the Master lowered their pipe. The moment the music ceased, a ripple went through the fae folk, and they surged forward to stand just behind their queen.

She held up one long-fingered hand, and her people stilled.

"Long and long have we searched for you, Elster," she said to the Master Piper. "Now your day of reckoning is at hand."

"I have committed no crime against the fae," the Master replied in a harsh, high voice reminiscent of a bird screeching.

"You have corrupted our magic with blood and death," the queen said, her voice hard. "There is a price to pay."

The Master Piper waved one black-gloved hand. "Paltry human lives, unwanted and unremarked. There is no cost to such as those."

Linnet's eyes widened at his words, the meaning becoming dreadfully clear. Blood and death. Unexplained disappearances among the children. The strange, painful magic of the Calling. She shuddered at the picture it painted.

The Strigosa Conservatory was far worse than any had guessed.

Except for the fae, who had come to punish Elster, whoever, or *what*ever, they might be.

"Twisted magic cannot be allowed to spread," the faerie queen said. "We have come to wipe the stain of you from the world."

The Master Piper laughed, a rattling caw. "You cannot stop me. Return to your own realm, or it will be *you* who disappears from memory."

"That realm was once yours," the queen replied. "And we will not allow you to continue on this path."

In an instant, a glittering sword was in her hand. She brought it down upon the Master Piper, who parried it with their pipe.

"Play!" the Master called, raising one arm and gesturing to the Pipers.

The drums started immediately, and the lutes. A few of the pipe players began the refrain of the Calling, and the fae folk flinched away, back toward the gate.

The queen struck again, but the Master Piper pivoted away, eluding her like smoke.

Piper Amalia resumed the counter-melody, and Linnet wanted to rush forward and dash the violin from her teacher's hands—but already the music was sapping her strength.

Then the Master Piper began to play once more; a harsh, rending melody that fell upon the fae folk like a razored whip.

The bright form of the queen dimmed, her sword-arm trembling. She turned her narrow face toward the cloisters, directly to where Linnet huddled against the wall. Even at that distance, Linnet could see the entreaty in her eyes.

Before she was overwhelmed by the dark music, Linnet

thrust off her robe. Her violin felt heavy as lead as she lifted it to her shoulder, the bow a length of iron bar.

In the courtyard, one of the bone-white maidens lay broken on the stones, and many of the fae staggered about as if mortally wounded. The music was killing them.

No. She could not let the Pipers win.

Clenching her teeth, Linnet dragged her bow across the D string. At first only a rough croak emerged, as if in parody of the first time she'd attempted to play. Faster, then. She pulled the bow back and forth, back and forth, letting the open string sound louder, clearer, pushing back against the dark magic of the Master Piper.

Some of the fae straightened and drew their own weapons, but then the Pipers redoubled their playing, and they faltered once more.

Play the song, Linnet urged her fingers. Her mind could not hold the melody clearly, not while the Master's music tainted the air.

But her fingers remembered. They *must.*

First the D, then up a fourth. Flurry down, ascend and echo. At first, she stumbled, but the further into the melody she played, the steadier it became.

A sweet humming filled the air, a descant almost above human hearing, and Linnet realized it was coming from the queen. She stood, sword held across her body, head thrown back, and song poured off her, bright magic that could only fly against the Pipers if a mortal gave it wings.

Linnet understood all this in a flash, and that she must close the distance between them. Still playing, she moved forward.

The first step was like pushing through a sucking bog.

The second, a searing fire.

The third was bitter ice—but Linnet kept going, the faerie music singing from her violin, her eyes fixed on the golden faerie queen.

The fae folk regrouped, some even leaping to pull the instruments from the Piper's hands. Yet even as the accompaniment fell away, the Master Piper continued to play, that dire sound now infused with unmistakable anger.

Three paces lay between Linnet and the queen.

All the winters in the world howled around her, but Linnet clung to her frozen bow and forced her fingers, and her feet, to move.

Two paces.

A thousand scorching desert winds flayed her, sucking the moisture from her body, but she pressed her fingers to the burning strings of her violin and kept on.

One pace.

The dead surrounded her, rising from the noxious muck that held her feet fast. Mama, Papa, reaching for her, begging for aid.

Tallia.

No! Linnet choked back her despair, though her tears fell like rain, staining the bright polish of her instrument, and her bow trembled.

Take heart. It was a warm whisper, barely heard, but it was enough.

She took the final step, and the Master Piper shrieked with rage. The sound blended with the skree of the pipes, a hideous, brutal howl that shook the night.

The queen raised her golden sword once more.

"I unmask you, Elster!" she cried. "Your power is stripped

from you, and from all those who thought to follow your path. Evermore, you shall be naught but a shadow of your former self, cursed to wander the world until you have saved thrice the number of lives you took."

She brought the sword down on the hooded figure of the Master Piper. The robes parted, fluttering like dark wings to reveal a creature that once might have been one of the fae.

It lifted clawed hands and hissed in fury, revealing sharp teeth between bloodless lips. Eyes like black pits set in a pale, narrow face, it lurched forward—

The queen's sword cleaved downward, putting an end to the creature.

Linnet flinched back, but there was no blood, no spatter of gore. Instead, a bird exploded upward from where the Master had stood, in a flurry of black and white wings. It squawked furiously, circled the queen three times, then flew away into the night.

As it passed over the gates of the Strigosa Conservatory, the entire front wall shuddered. With a sound like thunder, the stones and iron gates disintegrated into dust.

In the aftermath, silence descended. The Queen of the Fae closed her eyes, a terrible weariness on her face, then opened them again. Her glowing sword was gone, its power consumed in transforming the Master Piper from fell creature to harmless magpie.

"Who…" Linnet let out a shaky breath, then finished the question. "Who was Elster?"

"He was my consort, once," the queen said, her voice low and mournful. "But the power grew misshapen within him. He left my court, and for too long I did not know what had become of him."

"Is he defeated for good, now?"

"Indeed." The bleakness left the queen's expression as she glanced down at Linnet. "Without your aid, I fear we would not have been victorious. For that help, I grant you a boon."

"A boon?" Linnet felt as though she'd fallen into an enchanted tale, and didn't know how to extricate herself. Bargains with the fae were dangerous—she knew that much.

"Anything your heart desires." The queen gestured, and suddenly the air was filled with orange and black butterflies.

One alighted on the end of Linnet's bow, and she stared at it a long moment. Around them, the fae folk gathered their wounded, took up the body of the dancing maiden and bore it away.

The Pipers milled in the cloisters, their expressions dazed. A dozen goblins kept them penned there, presumably until the queen decided what to do with them.

The handful of orphans gathered by the Calling huddled by the remaining wall, darting confused, wondering glances at the fae and their queen.

Linnet shook her bow and the butterfly took flight once more, a speck of orange against the starry sky. Her heart's desire...

"I need to find my sister," she said at last.

"It is too simple a request," the queen said. "I can tell you she dwells within the Grand Burgher's house—but that is not payment enough."

"It is, to me," Linnet said.

"Kind must be returned in kind," the queen said. "I shall return at noon three days hence to hear your answer."

She turned away and floated gently over to the Pipers.

"You shall forget the creature called the Master Piper," she crooned, waving her arms in swooping arcs. Glittering dust fell over the Pipers, and they ceased muttering.

"The Strigosa Conservatory is nothing more than a place where human music is taught," she continued in her singsong tone. "The gates will not be rebuilt, and anyone wishing to leave may do so. Now go, sleep, and when you wake, your lives will be built anew."

Moving as though in a trance, the Pipers marched obediently through the cloister doors and disappeared into the conservatory.

"What about them?" Linnet dared to ask, gesturing to the orphans.

"Fear not for them, or any others within these walls," the queen said. "Yet, lend me the magic of your playing once more, ere I grow too weary."

Linnet was exhausted, herself, but one did not deny the Queen of the Fae. She lifted her violin and, once more, played the sweet, haunting notes of the faerie song.

The queen rose high into the air, until she almost seemed one of the glimmering stars. As Linnet poured the notes from her violin, the faerie wove back and forth over the whole of the conservatory. Sparkling dust fell like enchanted snow, covering the ugliness that had lain within.

One of the matrons bustled into the courtyard, clucking with concern, and gathered the orphan children to follow her back to the kitchens for a nice warm bite of bread.

The cistern fashioned to burn roaches transformed, elongating into a graceful marble fountain where water, not oil, splashed into the basin. The insects themselves turned to an elaborate design of vines and flowers worked into the stone.

The rats... well, rats are not so easily turned from one

thing into another, though some of them shrank to become mice, and others sprouted wings and went to join the flocks of pigeons.

As Linnet watched them fly away, the queen landed softly on the flagstones.

"What about the next infestation of rats?" Linnet asked. "How will the city manage without the Pipers?" Much as she'd hated the conservatory, they had provided a crucial service to Hamelin.

The queen gave Linnet a pitying look. "The rats were never disposed of. After every Calling, the Pipers simply let them back out into the city."

Appalled, Linnet blinked at her. "Why would they do such a thing?"

"Humans are oft ruled by greed. If they truly rid the city of rats, then what would happen to their flow of golden coin?"

Linnet could make no response to this. Nor could she speak of the greater evil the Master Piper had performed. If there ever had been a dark place of sacrifice beneath the cellars of the conservatory, she prayed that the queen's magic had erased it.

In the east, a faint wash of light picked out the silhouettes of steeples and towers against the sky. A bell rang, the sound reassuringly human after the eldritch music of the night.

"Rest, child." The Queen of the Fae placed one hand on Linnet's head, her touch light as a breath of wind. "Look for us in a thrice."

Then, in a whirl of light, she was gone, and all her folk with her.

The courtyard stood deserted, open to the city on one side. The Master Piper was defeated, and everything had changed.

How much, Linnet could not yet guess, but the morning would tell, soon enough.

Wearily, she cradled her violin in her arms, and stumbled away to seek her bed.

THE NEXT DAY, Linnet discovered that the Strigosa Conservatory had become simply a school of music for talented orphans, as well as a place that trained children for paid employment in service to the wealthy houses. None within the walls, or without, remembered the dire Master Piper, the magic of the Calling, or anything that had come before.

The teachers, no longer known as Pipers, were paid by a consortium of nearby towns, who in turn expected free concerts at all public events. It was a satisfactory bargain for all involved—although some of the instructors remained rather harsh in their methods.

Still, no orphans were beaten, nor servants either.

Linnet was expected to appear as usual for her lesson, and Teacher Amalia was as dour and uncomplimentary as ever. But instead of dreadful, soul-crushing music, Linnet discovered she had been given a variety of music, both solo and orchestral.

The shielded practice rooms were no longer lit by strange silver light, but were simply places where students might work on their music.

Still, she did not play the faerie song where anyone might hear.

That afternoon after that last, dreadful Calling, she went

to the servant's entrance of the Grand Burgher's house and asked if she might visit her sister.

Would Tallia even remember what had happened?

The woman who answered the door bade her wait, and went to fetch her sister. Linnet twisted her fingers together in hope, and worry.

"Linnet?" Tallia rushed to the threshold, then halted a pace from Linnet, one hand on the doorframe.

She wore a russet dress with green embroidery at the sleeves, and her hair was pulled back with filigreed barrettes. The look in her eyes was wary, and Linnet realized with a shock that her sister was nearly as tall as she.

"Tallia." She opened her arms and leaned forward, but her sister shrank back from her embrace.

"Why did you not come?" Tallia's voice shook, then gained in strength. "Three years, and you never visited! I despaired, Linnet. I waited and waited for you."

"I could not." Linnet dropped her arms, suddenly cold. Was this the price of the faerie song?

"*Would* not, you mean." Betrayal shone from her sister's eyes. "Everyone knows that students can come and go—it's not as if you were imprisoned in the conservatory."

Oh, but I was. Linnet swallowed the words. The past had changed, and she was the only one who had not changed with it. There was no use trying to explain; she could see Tallia would not believe her.

"Come with me," she said, instead.

"With you?" Tallia looked her up and down, the beginning of scorn on her face. "To where? I have no talent for music, as you may recall, and no desire to reduce my station by becoming simply a servant. I have a place in this household—a good place."

"But we could be together," Linnet said, faltering.

It was all she'd ever wanted. It was what she had promised. But now that she could keep that promise, it turned out that, for Tallia, it had been broken years ago.

"Together?" Tallia stepped back. "I am companion to the Grand Burgher's daughter now. And a better sister than you'll ever be."

"Tallia," Linnet entreated, holding out her hands as tears gathered in her eyes. "Please."

Her sister shook her head. "Go away! I don't want to see you again."

"But—"

Tallia shut the door in Linnet's face, leaving her alone with a heart turned to stone.

Blindly, she turned away from the well-appointed house with bright flowers in the window boxes. Turned away from her sister, lost to her because of the fae.

She'd wondered what to ask of the queen, but the choice now was simple.

AT NOON on the third day, Linnet waited in the courtyard of the Strigosa Conservatory. In one hand she held her violin case, in the other a small bag packed with a change of clothing and a loaf of bread. She didn't know if she would need them, where she was going, but it seemed best to be prepared.

As the bells struck twelve, the Queen of the Fae came, alighting in a golden blaze in the center of the flagstones.

None of the denizens of the conservatory paid any heed, simply going about their duties. Linnet glanced at their unheeding faces, then turned back to the queen.

"Can you make my sister love me again?" she asked, fearing the answer.

The faerie gave her a long, sorrowful look. "Alas, we may not meddle in the will of humans. Ask another boon, that I may grant it."

Linnet swallowed back her grief. There was a chance, just one...

"Will you allow me to Call, and see if she will come?"

The faerie queen's expression hardened. "I will not allow that dire music to enter the world once more."

"Not that," Linnet hastened to explain. "But... you did not take the power of the faerie song from me. At least not yet. With your help, could we not play a new music? One that would gather in only those who wanted to come?" *Please, let Tallia be one.*

The Queen of the Fae tilted her head, considering. Her bright hair waved about her, moved by unseen currents, and her glimmering wings fluttered idly.

"And then where would they go, these children who came willingly?" she asked.

"Somewhere better." Linnet waved at the conservatory, the city beyond. "Someplace filled with magic."

"You would enter my realm, then?"

"If you promise to treat us kindly."

There was nothing left for Linnet in the human world, after all. And she had come to realize over the past three days that she did not want to give up the one thing she still had: the bright magic of the faerie song. If the queen took the music away, back into her lands, then Linnet wanted to go with it.

There was still that one chance of happiness, too.

If Tallia heeded the Call and chose to answer, then they would go together into that magical realm. With the queen's help, Linnet would pour her whole heart into the song, all her love for her sister. It might be enough.

"Any who willingly follow this Call will be welcome in the lands beyond," the queen said. "No harm will come to you, nor unkindness—I give my solemn vow. But are you certain this is the boon you crave?"

"Yes."

"Then let us sing one last song into the mortal world, ere we depart."

Linnet nodded, then took her violin and bow from the case and began to play. The melody was a blend of the Calling and the faerie song—a yearning ache, holding out a promise that would not, this time, be broken.

Sweetly, softly, the Queen of the Fae joined in, weaving brightness and hope into the flow of notes.

Three times through Linnet played the music, each time braiding her fierce devotion to her sister into the threads of melody. Low, then high, then a fluttering echo back down. *I love you, Tallia. I miss you. I'm sorry.*

The children came, gathering in the open plaza. Some were dressed in rags, some in fine clothing. Some bore the welts of beatings, others, invisible scars inflicted by word and deed. Some were small of stature, some nearly full grown.

But all of them carried the hope in their eyes that now, things would be better. That there was, finally, a way out.

As she drew the faerie song to a close, Linnet scanned the

faces of the two score children who had answered the Call. Her heart caught when she saw a girl in a russet dress—but it was not Tallia.

None of them were. Her choice had been made.

Heart breaking, Linnet took the bow from the strings and lowered her violin.

"Mortals," the queen said, her voice warm and lilting, "do you freely choose to come with me into the bright land under the hill?"

"Yes!" they cried, with one voice.

"Then come." The queen nodded to Linnet. "Play us home."

Tears running silver down her cheeks, Linnet lifted her instrument and strode forward, letting a new melody form beneath her fingers. Letting a new path unfurl beneath her feet.

Each choice freely made—the beauty and heartbreak of a mortal life.

The Queen of the Fae soared ahead, and Linnet led the children out of the city, the music lilting behind them like a banner lifted by the wind.

～

ESCAPE

A LIZA ROTH ADVENTURE

THE SMELL of hyperfuel hung in the air as Liza Roth waited to board the shuttle from Turmeric Central to the inner system spaceport. The terminal here was quiet—a way station for luxury cruise liners looking for local color, a stopping place for those craving adventure, but not too much of it.

Starhub Station was where she'd find the rattle and whoosh, the frantic bustle of passengers and crew hurrying between flights. And it was where she'd find her next ship, bound for... well, she wasn't actually sure where. Just that her time of sanctuary in the Temple of Vishnu was over.

Amethyst-colored eyes looked up at her through the plas-mesh bag she was carrying.

"Mrow," the cat inside said, as though in agreement that it was time they moved on.

"At least I don't have to smuggle you under my shirt this time," Liza agreed. That hadn't been a comfortable trip—for either of them.

But the priests of Vishnu, in addition to being devout holy men, had some of the best nanotech in the galaxy. Through their connections, they'd procured traveling documents for Shade as a licensed animal companion, with all the required shots and scans.

It helped that Shade was no ordinary cat. Once, she'd been the pet of some pampered lady of Quality. The genetic modification of her feathery wings—as smoke-colored as the rest of her—was evidence enough of that. Nightshade, as Liza had named her, was a high-class feline.

In addition to papers for Shade, the priests had given Liza several holo-IDs, with identities ranging from scullery maid to mid-level noble. For this trip out, Liza had chosen that of a tourist, one of those slightly eccentric lady travelers who took a notion to jaunt unaccompanied about the star systems.

Well, unaccompanied other than their pets.

She shifted, wishing she'd chosen to travel under a different identity. The woolen walking dress she'd donned for the role of lady adventurer was too hot and scratchy for standing about in the afternoon sun.

The shuttle doors slid open. Liza took one last breath of the dry, spice-scented air and glanced over her shoulder at the tall domes of the Temple of Vishnu. They rose, white and shining, over the dun-colored quarters of the city. Her home for almost a year.

"Thank you," she said quietly, though she'd already said her goodbyes, and there was no one to hear this last farewell.

When she'd first claimed refuge at the temple, a fugitive from the Galactic Nobility, the priests had set her to earning her keep by sweeping the temple and changing the huge tubs of incense. Later, once she'd stopped looking over her shoulder for bounty hunters or her father's mercenaries, the priests had asked her to help advise them on political matters.

Wise of them, considering she'd been raised in the top strata of the nobility, in a household full of political machinations. Liza let out a sigh. Not to put too fine a point on it, she had once been a princess.

And then a miner, an itinerant musician, a maid—jobs that let her put food in her mouth, clothes on her back, and stay off the radar of anyone searching for her. She hadn't expected to become a temple acolyte, but the star winds blew where they may.

The priests had welcomed her to stay longer, but an itchy restlessness had taken hold of her in recent weeks.

"You're sure there are no bounty hunters waiting to snatch me the moment I set foot outside the temple?" she'd asked the old priest who'd befriended her.

"There is no certainty," he'd said. "But our intel shows no recent activity on Turmeric Central regarding your whereabouts."

The implication was clear, however. Once she stepped off the planet, who knew what might be waiting for her?

"I'll take my chances," she'd said.

"Hm." The old man pursed his mouth and looked at her. "Even with six million on your head, and a land grant? You could remain here—your sparring skills need work."

She'd given him a tight grim. "And earn more bruises from you?"

For such an elderly-seeming fellow, the priest was surprisingly spry. He'd taught her the rudiments of an ancient earth form of martial arts called jujitsu and, while she'd mastered the basics, there was plenty more to learn.

"I can't stay." She'd shrugged in apology. "There's more in

the galaxy for me than spending the rest of my life at the Temple of Vishnu. Delightful though it is."

The lofty, incense-filled main temple held a pervasive sense of peace, and she would always treasure her time there. But the universe called.

In fact, the shuttle was boarding now.

"All passengers, proceed up the ramp," a tinny voice announced. "Shuttle A-4, en route to Starhub Station. We depart promptly at half past the hour."

The British Galactic Empire ran on a strict schedule, and woe to anyone running late. Promptness and efficiency were prized, and transports waited for no one. A fact that had enabled Liza to escape from Earth, jumping on a ship at the last possible moment ahead of her pursuers. Even her father's status as the Duke of Albany and Xersis-9 hadn't been enough to turn the transport around.

Now, though, she was Mrs. Rothbotham (a silly name, in her opinion, but the priests had chosen her false identities without consulting her) traveling about the system with her feline companion.

The flight attendants waved her aboard, with only a cursory glance at Shade's carrying case. It was assumed, correctly, that anyone traveling with an animal would ensure said creature provided no disruption—at risk of their pet being confiscated.

Liza wondered how many animals had been taken from their owners, and if they languished in various station holding pens. She told herself they must all be adopted, eventually.

Perhaps my new career is a vigilante animal-rescuer. Although she hardly needed to draw more attention to herself.

As if sensing her thoughts, Shade began to purr loudly.

Even when Liza stowed her beneath the seat, the throaty vibration didn't cease.

"A kitty, is it?" The rotund fellow seated next to her inserted his monocle and leaned forward to look at Shade. "They purr when afraid, don't you know."

"Indubitably," Liza murmured.

No point in arguing with the fellow. He seemed only a few years older than herself, but his pompous air made him seem twice that age.

"Travelled much, miss?" He turned his gaze to her.

The monocle distorted his right eye, making him resemble an inquisitive goldfish. Despite his open expression, Liza felt a stab of distrust. He seemed pleasant enough, but she was wary of too many questions.

"It's Mrs.," she informed him primly. "Mrs. Rothbotham."

He frowned and glanced at her left hand, probably to ascertain whether or not she wore a ring. But Liza's brown leather travelling gloves were a useful concealment. She folded her hands in her lap and gave him a bland smile.

"Pleasure to meet you." His curiosity foiled, he dipped his head politely. "I'm Squire Kenwick. And where are you off to, Mrs. Rothbotham?"

"Oh." She waved her hand airily. "Anywhere of interest, I suppose."

"Be careful of the jungles of Dedrem," he said. "The indigenous flora might eat your cat."

Liza shot him a look. Was the squire teasing her, or had he spoken the words in earnest?

"That planet is not on my itinerary," she said.

As the shuttle lifted from Turmeric Central, she turned to look out the grainy window, the thick plasglass pitted by the impact of tiny space debris. She glimpsed one last flash of white from the temple domes, and then the transport accelerated starward. The pressure pushed her back into the seat. Shade stopped purring.

"We'll be free of the thrust soon," the squire said, as though Liza had never set foot on a ship in her life.

She gave him a nod, mentally going through the list of peerage that had been drilled into head when she was younger. The title of Squire Kenwick wasn't known to her, but then, she'd only needed to memorize the ranks of the upper gentry. Judging from the man's demeanor and garb he was comfortably well off, but not anyone with clout in the nobility.

The squire narrated the entire trip, pointing out the nearby planets and lecturing her on proper emergency procedures and the location of the suits.

Luckily, it was a short flight.

He patted her arm reassuringly as they descended.

"Once we land, do you need any assistance getting about the station?" he asked.

Liza studied his expression, seeing nothing but a genuine, if misguided, desire to help.

"Thank you," she said, "but no. I can manage quite well on my own."

"Very well." He looked a bit crestfallen. Perhaps he didn't quite know what to do with himself, either.

The attendants called for everyone to make ready to disembark. The squire donned his bowler hat, and Liza retrieved Shade from her spot beneath the seat. Purple eyes gazed at her reproachfully. It was clear the cat was more than ready to be freed from her carrier.

"Soon," Liza promised.

"I say!" Squire Kenwick was regarding Shade with a look of surprise. "Your cat has wings."

"Yes." Liza didn't elaborate.

"Can it fly, then, or are they just decorative?"

"She's capable of flying." No need to let him know that Shade was as comfortable in the air as she was on the ground.

"I've never considered getting a modified pet before," he said. "But a flying cat, that's capital. Expensive though, I'd think."

"Mm. Oh look, the line's moving." Liza stepped into the aisle. "Good day, sir. It was a pleasure making your acquaintance."

"Likewise, likewise." He doffed his bowler.

It didn't take long to disembark from the shuttle. Liza kept her pace brisk, giving the appearance that she knew where she was going, and let the throng at the dock absorb her.

The squire caught up to her at the flight schedule holo-board, however. Liza pretended not to notice him standing at her shoulder as she studied the possible flights out. Where would she go? She'd best choose, and soon.

A commotion caught her attention. She glanced over, to see a muscled, hard-faced woman pushing her way through the crowd. Straight toward Liza.

The woman glanced down at her handheld, then back to her, a gleam in her eyes. She gave a single, sharp nod.

Confound it! A bounty hunter—and already on her trail. Heart hammering, Liza took a step back, preparing to flee.

"I don't think so," a deep voice said.

A meaty hand grabbed her shoulder and swung her around to face an immensely tall man.

"Looks like we got us a prize," he said.

Shade let out a hiss, the fur of her tail bristling up through the mesh of her carrier.

"Unhand the lady," Squire Kenwick said, though his voice shook.

Liza couldn't fight; not carrying her valise and Shade.

"Here," she cried, thrusting the carrier at the squire, then dropping her valise.

She grasped the bounty hunter's arm with both hands and pulled, but there was no leverage for her to use against him. He stood rooted like a tree, holding her fast and laughing at her efforts.

Then the woman arrived and, quick as a blink, clapped a pair of restraint bracelets around Liza's wrists.

"What is this nonsense?" the squire spluttered. "You can't just—"

"Galactic Enforcers," the woman said, flashing a badge that was likely counterfeited. "This young woman has a price on her head."

Damnation. Liza ground her teeth. She couldn't believe she'd been caught so easily. A year of living in safety had made her too soft.

Squire Kenwick took a step back, blinking at Liza. "I only just met her, I swear. I've nothing to do with it. Whatever it is."

Liza looked at him, widening her eyes in entreaty. She glanced down at the carrier, then back to him, hoping he could read her message. And that he'd take pity, if not on her, then on her cat.

The large man grinned. "If you do, we'll find out—never fear. Now hand over the carrier."

"Open it!" Liza yelled, then barreled forward, using her shoulders to force her way through the gathered onlookers.

Her blasted skirts hampered her movements, however, and she knew she couldn't escape—but that wasn't her aim. If she could create enough of a distraction…

The bounty hunters grabbed Liza, and the woman sent a stun-shock through her that made her stagger. She was well and truly caught, now.

With a yowl, Shade shot into the air, wings pumping furiously.

Thank you, Liza mouthed at the squire as the bounty hunters slung her back around.

"I couldn't help it," Squire Kenwick protested as the woman stalked over to him. "It ripped open the closure, see? And look at my hand! Nearly torn to shreds."

There was a single red line going down the back of his hand. It could have been made by a desperate cat—or the edge of a plasmetal zipper.

Shade, still meowing, flapped in circles over their heads. The tall bounty hunter jumped, but Shade was clever enough to soar out of reach.

He lunged again, and his female companion scowled at him. "Leave it. There's no mention of a cat."

"Look at it, though." He stared up at Shade. "That'd fetch a pretty penny."

"Not worth it. We've drawn too much attention already. Bring the girl." She pinned the squire with her gaze. "If we find you're involved, you're next."

He gulped, and refused to meet Liza's eyes. "I was just leaving."

"Good." The bounty hunter scooped up Liza's valise, her

companion scooped up Liza, and they quickly made for the nearest exit.

"Go," Liza called up at Shade, though her tongue was clumsy from the effects of the stun. "Don't follow me."

Her last sight was of the cat turning to wheel away, soaring high above the crowds until she was lost in the shadows.

THE BOUNTY HUNTERS took Liza to a cavernous warehouse full of cargo containers. She read the destination readouts as the man lugged her past: *Palatio*, *New Scotia*, and someplace simply designated as *TR-14*.

There was little hope that she might escape and smuggle herself out, unfortunately. In addition to the wrist restraints, the bounty hunters had fastened strictors around each ankle.

"Like having your feet cut off," she'd overheard an old miner say once, and it was true.

Even if she could somehow overpower her captors, she couldn't run. Crawl, maybe, but with her arms pinioned in front of her, it wasn't a very feasible idea. Plus, once she'd gained the corridors outside, it would be clear she was some kind of escapee.

Being picked up by redcoats wouldn't be any better than the bounty hunters. The end result would be the same— shipped back to Earth to face her family's justice.

She shivered at the thought. The duke would not go easy on his runaway daughter, despite the handful of years that had passed. Indeed, he would probably be all the angrier that she'd managed to avoid detection for so long. One did not lightly cross one of the highest-ranking men in the galaxy.

Still, after being deposited in a corner of the bounty hunters' makeshift camp, Liza couldn't help but watch, and try to plan. No matter how hopeless her chances.

Even if she could overpower her captors, the woman had the restraints keyed to her handheld. Which was retina-locked, so stealing it would be of no use.

The hours passed. The bounty hunters didn't bother feeding her, and Liza wondered what their plans were. Her father wanted her back alive, she was certain of it. Trying to find a comfortable position—hard to do when propped against a wall with useless limbs—she closed her eyes and pretended to sleep.

Perhaps she did sleep, for when she was next conscious, she realized the bounty hunters were talking.

"Transport's at oh-three-hundred," the man was saying. "They'll have a berth for us in Medical, as arranged. Should we put the girl on the medicot?"

"Not yet," his partner said. "There's only so much knockout in the IV. Don't want her coming to before we're on the ship."

The man snorted. "What's she going to do, even if she does wake up? Sic her killer cat on us?"

"That creature's long gone," the woman said.

I'm sorry, Shade, Liza thought, regret surging through her. *It's not the future I planned for us.* She hoped the cat would find a refuge somewhere. Maybe Squire Kenwick would take her in.

A faint movement overhead made her glance up to the high ceiling. Something fluttered in the shadows atop one of the metal girders, and her heartbeat thudded with hope. And worry.

If Shade had followed her, what could the cat possibly do? One small feline and one girl in restraints were not the most formidable of foes—especially against two hardened bounty hunters.

A shape glided from the girder to the top of a nearby shipping container. The silhouette was unmistakably that of a winged feline. *Oh, Shade, what are you up to?*

"What are you going to do with your half of the reward?" the male bounty hunter asked, but didn't wait for his partner to answer. "Me, I'm going to open a bar somewhere. Maybe on the planet they give us."

The woman let out a snort. "It won't be a planet, fool. Probably an over-mined hunk of moon that's no use to anyone."

Privately, Liza agreed with her. The nobility were good at making empty promises.

"Don't care," the man said. "It's got to be livable, right? I'll build a place, and people will come. Why, my bar could be the hub for mercs everywhere. I can see it now—*Lugash's Tavern*, in ten foot holo letters."

Big dreams, and for a moment Liza felt a bitter ache at the thought of all she'd lost.

Selina. The name echoed through her, though the searing pain had blunted a little, with time.

Being hauled back to Earth would be the death of everything they'd hoped for. Liza's heart twisted at the thought. She couldn't give up. Not yet.

Atop the container, Shade shifted.

"Hey," Liza said, hoping to distract her captors. "I'm thirsty."

"Same here." The man grinned. "A nice pint of Deneb, now—"

"You and your ale," the woman said, shaking her head. She grabbed a dented thermobottle and brought it to Liza. "No tricks."

Liza held up her bound wrists, illustrating her helpless position.

Eyes narrowed, the bounty hunter opened the lid, then, staying well back, handed it to Liza.

It was beyond awkward, trying to bring the bottle to her mouth with her arms restrained. For every sip Liza managed of the flat-tasting recycled water, she spilled twice as much on her woolen traveling dress.

Two pinpricks of bright purple shone from the dark atop the shipping container. Soft as a whisper, Liza heard the rustle of Shade's wings. Whatever foolish, ill-fated rescue attempt the cat planned, it was about to happen.

Liza took a last gulp of water, then made to hand the bottle back. At the last second, she flicked her wrists. The container clattered away, rolling in a lopsided arc over the stained concrete floor. A dribble of water left a dark line in its wake.

"Sorry," she said.

"You will be." The woman stalked over to retrieve her bottle.

If Liza hadn't been prepared, she never would have sensed Shade's attack. As it was, the cat glided overhead on silent wings. Something hung, glinting, at her neck. With one swift paw, she batted it to the floor, where it shattered in a tinkle of glass, right in front of the man. A faint yellow mist rose up.

"What the devil?" he exclaimed, bending over to examine the broken vial.

The woman strode over, caught a whiff of the mist, and backed hastily away. "Don't breathe it!"

Too late—at least for him. With a crash, the bounty hunter toppled over.

The woman whirled, stumbling slightly, and drew her taz-pistol.

"Come out," she called. "I know you're there, Vim. Trying to steal our catch, are you? Well, I won't stand for it!"

She wove back and forth on her feet, and Liza desperately hoped she wouldn't, in fact, stand much longer.

"Go for her eyes," somebody yelled in a shaking voice.

With a piercing yowl, Shade plummeted down, wings folded tightly against her body. She made straight for the bounty hunter's face, twisting to evade the taz bolts the woman shot at her.

A figure raced forward, and with surprise Liza saw it was Squire Kenwick, a stunrod in his hand. He took aim at the woman and fired a sizzling arc at her.

Liza grimaced as he missed, the edge of the stun just grazing the bounty hunter's shoulders. She whirled, teeth bared, and leveled her pistol at the squire.

No. Liza refused to let this rescue end in disaster.

She flung herself onto the cold floor, using that brief momentum to roll forward. Her arms ached and her feet, well, she hoped she wouldn't accidentally break her ankles.

With a thud, she collided against the bounty hunter's legs, just as the woman let out a bolt. It went wide, and she kicked Liza in the ribs.

"Stun her," Liza cried, gritting her teeth against the stab of pain.

"I'm trying." Squire Kenwick sounded on the verge of tears. "It has to recharge."

At least he had the sense to duck around the corner of the shipping container.

The bounty hunter aimed another kick at Liza, but she managed to jackknife away before the boot landed in her ribs again.

"I'll deal with you, later." The woman glared at Liza, her voice harsh with rage. Then, pistol at the ready, she crept to the edge of the container.

"She's coming," Liza called.

Damnation. How long did that stun rod take to prime, anyway? What a useless weapon.

The bounty hunter leaped around the corner, firing, and Liza bit her lip. She wouldn't put her credits on Squire Kenwick in this fight, unfortunately.

Speaking of whom, he crept around the far side of the container. The stun rod trembled in his hands, and he shot Liza an agonized look.

Overhead, Shade let out a yowl, her gaze fixed on the corner where the bounty hunter had disappeared. Urgently, Liza jerked her head at the squire to get back under cover. If the stakes weren't so high, the whole thing would have been amusing, in a darkly comic way.

The bounty hunter sidled around the edge of the container. She frowned when she saw that Squire Kenwick had given her the slip.

Clank. Something shifted atop the container. The woman glanced up, then yelled and dodged out of the way as a metal bar plummeted down, smacking the concrete where she'd just been standing.

Shade crouched atop the container, peering down like a petite gargoyle.

"Damned cat," the bounty hunter said, lifting her pistol to fire at Shade.

"Look out," Liza called.

The air lit with the blue taz bolt, just as Squire Kenwick barreled back around the corner, stun rod glowing. With a determined expression, he pointed it at the bounty hunter and fired.

This time, the arc connected, and the woman slumped unconscious to the floor, pistol clattering from her grasp.

With a graceful swoop, Shade left her perch and landed delicately on the ground, putting herself between the bounty hunter and her gun.

"Oh, well done," Liza said. "The both of you."

"Mrow." Shade sounded rather pleased with herself.

Squire Kenwick wiped his perspiring forehead with the back of his sleeve. "I wasn't sure we could do it, frankly."

Neither had Liza, but she didn't stop smiling. "Grab that pistol, then let's get me out of these restraints before the bounty hunters wake up."

"How?" The squire scooped up the gun, then came to stand beside her.

"The woman's handheld—there, clipped to her belt. When you turn it on, you'll have to pry open one of her eyelids for the retinal scan. Oh, and put your stun rod next to me. Just in case." She wasn't sure she could operate it, bound as she was, but she felt better with a weapon nearby.

With a look of distaste, Squire Kenwick went over to the

bounty hunter. The woman had fallen facing Liza, and it was unnerving to see her blank stare as the squire held her lid open and waved the handheld in front of her face.

For a tense moment, nothing happened. Liza frantically tried to come up with a plan. Her brain felt like an asteroid knocked out of orbit, helplessly spinning in freefall.

Then the handheld beeped, the screen blossomed with text, and Liza released her breath.

"There should be an icon for the strictors," Liza said. "A snake, I think."

Squire Kenwick frowned, then nodded. "There is it. Let me see... *release*, that ought to do it."

With a snick, the bindings around her ankles loosened. Liza waved her legs, trying to kick off the strictors. Her feet still felt like they were missing.

"Hold on, let me help you," he said.

"Just get my wrists loose." Now that she was almost free, she was panicking; the fear that she'd held at bay rising up to swamp her.

As if sensing Liza's distress, Shade came up and bumped her mistress on the cheek with her cold nose.

It helped. Liza closed her eyes, forced her racing heartbeat and panting breaths to slow. They would get out of this. They would.

"Almost there," Squire Kenwick said.

Her wrist restraints clicked off, and she gasped with the pain of sensation returning to her arms.

The male bounty hunter groaned and began to stir. Without hesitation, Liza grabbed the stun rod. It took a second for her nerveless fingers to find the button, but when she did, she shot the man solidly in the side. He subsided into unconsciousness once more.

"We need to get out of here," Liza said. "Help me stand."

It was easier said than done, however. Her feet were blocks of lead, and even with Squire Kenwick supporting her, she couldn't walk.

"Put me back down," she said after several awkward attempts.

"Whatever are we to do now?" he asked, helping prop her against the wall. "I'm afraid I haven't the strength to carry you."

"I know." She pursed her mouth, trying to think. The bounty hunters had a plan... "Search for a medicot. We can put me on that, and wheel me out. It should be nearby."

He gave her a dubious look, but went to look.

Shade had disappeared again, but now let out an imperative meow. Squire Kenwick hurried toward the sound, ducked behind another stack of containers, then reappeared wheeling the cot. Shade sat in the center of it, looking smug.

Liza was glad to see her valise tucked in the rack beneath the cot. At least she hadn't lost all her worldly possessions, although almost everything could be replaced.

Everything, except Selina's portrait.

"Here we go," the squire said, bringing the medicot to where Liza sat.

He levered it down as low as it would go, then gave her an apologetic look.

"Well, let's get me on the blasted thing," she said.

After some awkward maneuvering, they managed to get her installed in the cot. Shade hovered overhead, keeping an eye on the proceedings.

Squire Kenwick eyed the prone forms of the bounty hunters. "Should we stun them again?"

"Probably." The last thing they needed was for her assailants to recover and chase them down.

She pulled out the stun rod, delivering half a charge to each of the bounty hunters. They didn't have time to wait for the blasted thing to fully recharge, after all.

As soon as she finished, the squire rapidly wheeled Liza to the warehouse exit. A small trunk sat beside the door, and he paused to hoist it under the cot, next to Liza's valise.

"Just in case, I brought my luggage," he said. "I thought, in the unlikely even we succeeded in the rescue, we might need to make a quick getaway.

"Good thinking." It seemed the squire did have a modicum of sense, after all.

As they stepped into the station corridors, Shade landed on the cot and burrowed under the covers at Liza's side. Against impossible odds, they'd freed her from the bounty hunters, and the enormity of it washed over her.

"Good kitty." Blinking back tears, she gave Shade a pat.

"A sight more than good," Squire Kenwick said. "That is the most amazing feline I've ever had the pleasure of meeting."

At his words, Shade began to purr.

"She is," Liza agreed, though she herself hadn't quite realized the depth of the cat's intelligence.

At the temple, Shade had seemed to understand when Liza spoke to her, and would occasionally let herself be directed. Once, she'd even flown to the top of the high ceiling and then batted at the small basket of marigold petals she carried about her neck, letting them cascade down in a shower of gold.

It was a trick the old priest had taught her. In retrospect,

Liza wondered if the old man knew how useful such a thing might be.

"How did you come up with this plan?" Liza asked. "And on such short notice?"

"Your cat found me, and wouldn't let me alone. She was making a spectacle of herself, and it was evident she wanted me to follow her. To keep her quiet, I did. She led me to an apothecary shop, marched along the counter as pretty as you please, and set her paw on that vial of knockout."

"You are a marvel," Liza said to the lump nestled beside her.

Shade's purring intensified.

"It took me some time to understand that she wanted me to fasten the vial about her neck," Squire Kenwick admitted. "By then, I knew I had to find a weapon of some sort."

"Why a stun rod?"

"It was the only thing I had enough credits for," he said sheepishly.

Touched, Liza glanced at him. "You spent all your credits for this?"

"I'll be able to get more." He sounded a bit unsure of the fact, however. "And it was for a worthy cause, indeed."

"And I thank you for your efforts on my behalf, good sir."

No doubt Squire Kenwick thought of himself as her knight errant now. Unfortunate, as her life demanded she be as unencumbered as possible.

Although—without Shade and the well-meaning squire, she'd still be in the tender clutches of the bounty hunters. Perhaps a bit of encumbrance wasn't such a bad thing, after all.

He paused as the corridor they'd been traversing ended in a T. "Now where?"

Where indeed? They had to get off the station as soon as possible.

"What time is it?"

Squire Kenwick pulled out his pocket watch and glanced down, the glowing numbers shedding blue light over his features. "Half past two."

Liza rolled on her side, her feet clunking uselessly at the end of her legs, and pulled out her tablet. Quickly, she found the station network and brought up the list of imminent departures.

"Berth 142," she said. It was the only transport leaving at the top of the hour. "Turn right."

"What ship is it, and bound where?"

"The *Kisa*, headed to Alpha Centauri." A bit too close to Earth for her liking, but it was the only option. Beggars, choosers, and all that. "We'll take the passage the bounty hunters arranged, and be long gone by the time they wake. That is, if you agree..."

She trailed off, studying Squire Kenwick's round, jovial face. He'd been pulled into her mess and, despite everything, had helped save her. It was unfair of her to expect him to continue to be embroiled in her troubles.

"Are you suggesting leaving me behind?" He looked so offended at the notion, she couldn't help but smile.

"Once I'm aboard, you needn't accompany me any further. Perhaps you'd prefer to make other arrangements."

He winced slightly. "I haven't the means, currently. And although you seem to be a somewhat capable young lady, I can't leave you to make your way, unescorted and wounded. Especially with such unsavory characters after you."

He glanced over his shoulder, as if expecting to see the bounty hunters in hot pursuit.

Shade made a little chirp of agreement, and that settled the matter.

Liza knew she had some explaining to do. Luckily, their arrival at Berth 142 took precedence.

"Medical bay doors," she said in a low voice, nodding to the aft of the ship. "Just bluster on through. I need to play unconscious."

His ruddy cheeks paling, he nodded at her. "Did they give any names? The bounty hunters, I mean."

She thought back. "Lugash, I think the man was called. If they ask for a password, try *ale*."

"Ale? As in beer?"

Liza nodded. "Good luck."

She let her head fall back and closed her eyes, trying to force some of the tension out of her body. It must have worked well enough, for the guard at the door paid her no mind.

"Lugash here," Squire Kenwick said, pitching his voice low and clipping his words. He didn't sound like a bounty hunter —but he didn't sound like a gentleman, either. "Need to board. With my cargo."

"Oh, aye? There's supposed to be two of you."

"New business came up. She made other plans off-station."

There was a pause, presumably as the guard accessed his screen. Liza didn't dare peek, though she desperately wanted to.

"You're approved," the guard said. "First bay on the left. And hurry it up—we depart in ten minutes."

None too soon.

The medicot lurched forward, the wheels clunking onto the rougher surface of the ship's floors. She heard the whoosh of a door opening, then closing.

"You can open your eyes," Squire Kenwick whispered.

"Don't forget to lock the door," she said, just as softly.

He pivoted, and a moment later the locking mechanism engaged.

"Should I put you in there?" he asked, nodding to the padded medical berth.

She let out a tiny shudder. "No—just lower the cot and we can put me in the extra jump seat. I'm starting to be able to feel my feet."

Hopefully, by the time they landed on Alpha Centauri, she'd be able to walk off the ship under her own power.

Though they struggled to get her out of the cot and buckled into the flight seat, it was easier than installing her on the medicot had been. Shade emerged from beneath the covers to watch, her eyes bright with interest. Liza belted in while the squire stored the cot in the hatch beneath the medical berth, and then made sure their luggage was secured.

"What about Princess?" he asked, taking the second seat.

"Princess?" For a frigid second, Liza thought he was referring to *her*, that somehow he'd discovered her true identity, and was simply picking up where the bounty hunters had left off.

Then he nodded to Shade, and she slumped in relief.

"Your cat," he said. "I didn't know what to call her."

"Shade. And I can hold her in my lap."

He nodded. "A fitting name. Though a bit practical, don't you think?"

"I am a practical woman," she replied.

"Are you, now?" He gave her a quizzical look. "What's all this business about, then? Bounty hunters after you and whatnot. Seems a bit irregular."

Liza petted Shade's feathery wings and launched into the story she'd come up with as they'd hurried to catch the *Kisa*.

"It's my uncle, Lord Farthingale. He doesn't believe I should be out traveling the galaxy on my own. I've been ignoring his summons to return, and apparently he engaged the bounty hunters to bring me back to Londinium."

The squire looked affronted. "That's not very gentlemanly of him! Why, those bounty hunters seemed more like ruffians than the types who could be trusted to escort a lady home."

"My uncle believes in expediency." She let out a sigh. "I suppose I ought to go sort matters out, however. There is nothing more ignominious than being dragged home by unsavory thugs."

A loud beep sounded in the room, then echoed down the corridor.

"Attention all decks. Prepare for our on-time departure to Alpha Centauri. Crew members, ensure that all passengers are securely harnessed."

Squire Kenwick sent her a worried glance. "Are they going to come and check on us?"

"No—I believe these seats are on auto-sensor. See the green light there? It shows that all occupants of this medical bay are safely belted in."

Shade let out a little chirp, and Liza glanced down, smiling. "Well, not *all* occupants. But the ones in the seats, at any rate."

"Stand by in three, two, one." The ship's announcement rang out, accompanied by a lurch and the sound of clanking metal. "Undocking complete."

Liza let out a breath and felt her shoulders relax. They'd made it off the station.

"I wish we had a window," Squire Kenwick said, a bit ruefully. "I like to see the stars."

"So do I." Liza shot him a companionable glance. "But once we're underway, it will probably be safe to go to the observation deck." And hopefully find a bit of something to eat.

And then?

The words she'd spoken earlier to the squire echoed through her. *There is nothing more ignominious than being dragged home by unsavory thugs.*

It was the absolute truth. And she was tired of running.

Perhaps it was time for Princess Elizabeth Calloway von Saxe-Roth to confront her family, and win her freedom once and for all. She owed herself, her companions—and most of all, her dreams—no less.

As if sensing her thoughts, Shade settled down in Liza's lap with a satisfied purr. Stroking the soft gray fur, Liza's conviction solidified. It wouldn't be easy, staying one step ahead of the bounty hunters, but she had fortitude, and allies. And a future waiting among the stars.

But first, it was time to go home.

AUTHOR'S NOTE

THIS STORY DRAWS on the Icelandic fairy tale *Kisa the Cat*, where an intrepid feline saves her princess mistress from a giant who kidnaps her and cuts off her feet. Although the cat in that tale cannot fly, she can perform magic, which is almost as good. If you'd like to read more about Liza's adventures, pick up *Comets & Corsets*, which includes three more stories detailing her history, including how she first meets Shade.

ABOUT THE AUTHOR

ANTHEA SHARP IS the *USA Today* bestselling author of the Feyland series, where faerie magic and high-tech gaming collide. In addition to the fae fantasy/cyberpunk mashup of Feyland, she also writes fantasy romance and Victorian Spacepunk set in the world of Victoria Eternal. Find out more at antheasharp.com and join her mailing list for a free story!

WALTZED

CHAPTER 1

LONDON, *May 1851*

THE SOFT GRAY drizzle of an English spring coated the half-open buds of the rhododendron flowers in the garden and glazed the windows of the late Viscount Tremont's town-house. His only daughter, Eleanor, however, was oblivious to the rain or the wet flowers or the chill in the library despite the coals on the hearth.

She had a thick woolen shawl tucked about her shoulders and was deeply engrossed in the adventures of David Copperfield. Like the hero of Dickens's latest novel, she, too, had known happiness as a child. And had subsequently been the unfortunate recipient of a stepfamily who was, as one might put it, less than kind.

"Ellie!" Her stepsister Abigail burst into the library. "Whatever are you doing in here?"

"Reading," Ellie said, marking the page number in her

mind with a silent sigh. She knew from experience that she would not return to her novel anytime soon.

Abigail tended to overexcitement, as redheads often did. Thankfully, she was not as spiteful as her older sister, especially when she and Ellie were alone. But whenever one of Ellie's stepsisters caught her reading, they found some reason to interrupt her—usually to put her to work.

"You must hurry up to your room," Abby said. "Your hair looks dreadful."

With some effort, Ellie kept herself from reaching to pat the bun at the back of her head. No doubt it was a bit messy, but she'd learned that any sign of weakness in front of her stepsiblings—or worse, her stepmother—would result in heapings of scorn.

"I'm not overly troubled about the state of my hair," she said. "After all, it's only me and Mr. Dickens." She lifted her book in emphasis.

Perhaps, this once, Abby would not insist that Ellie come untangle her hair ribbons or polish her jewelry or any of a thousand annoying little tasks, and Ellie might return to her novel in peace.

Abby made an exasperated noise. "But that's just it. You have a caller!"

"I what?" That was unexpected. Ellie never had callers. With a prickle of interest, she closed her book and laid it on the side table.

Was this a cruel trick or was Abby telling the truth? Her other stepsister, Delia, would certainly enjoy raising Ellie's hopes. It would be like her to send Ellie hurrying to her room to make herself presentable, then laughing when she entered the empty parlor to find no one awaiting her after all.

"I've been trying to tell you." Abby crossed her arms. "Why don't you ever listen? No wonder Mama is always displeased with you."

Privately, Ellie thought the source of that displeasure had more to do with her existence as the late viscount's only child and the discovery that Papa had apparently left a much smaller fortune than expected upon his death. Not enough to keep a viscountess and her daughters in any kind of style, as her stepmother often reminded her—as if it were Ellie's fault that her father had not, in fact, been as well-off as they had all thought.

Oh, Papa.

Tears threatened to clog her throat, and she swallowed them back.

"Hurry!" Abby said, tapping her foot. "You oughtn't keep him waiting too long."

"Who is it?"

"A gentleman—I didn't recognize him."

"And he asked for me?" Perhaps it had something to do with Papa's estate, although any solicitor would call upon her stepmother and not Ellie. And besides, all that had been settled months ago.

"I heard him ask for you specifically," Abby said, a hint of contempt in her voice. "But if you'd rather not believe me and prefer to make a fool of yourself . . ."

"Very well," Ellie said. "Tell Mr. Atkins—"

"Miss Eleanor," the butler said from the threshold, as if summoned by the mention of his name. "You have a caller. I've put him in the front parlor."

Abby shot her a scathing look. "I don't know why I even bother with you, Ellie."

With that, she tossed her head and whisked out of the room, nearly running over the portly Mr. Atkins in the process.

He hastily stood aside, then nodded at Ellie. "I'll tell Lord Newland you'll be down shortly?"

"Please do."

She'd no notion who Lord Newland might be, unless he were somehow related to the Newland family she'd known several years ago. Papa and Mr. Newland had been fast friends until the family had left for India. She'd exchanged letters with Kit, the son, for nearly two years until their correspondence trailed off into silence.

In truth, for quite a while she'd cherished notions of marrying the black-haired boy who'd been such a merry companion in her youth. Even after they'd removed to India, she spent time reading about the country and daydreaming about living in that bright and exotic land, Kit at her side.

Then Papa had remarried Lady Tremont, which had been somewhat trying. Not much later, he'd died, and nothing mattered anymore—except battling through the fog of grief surrounding her. And running to do her stepfamily's bidding, which only amplified her misery.

As soon as the butler left the library, Ellie glanced at her reflection in the mirror over the mantel. Oh dear—Abby had been correct. Her pale hair was straggling out of her bun, a hairpin hanging from one of the fine strands like some strange spider over her shoulder.

There was a smudge of soot on her cheekbone, ashy against the pallor of her complexion. She glanced down at her wrist to see a matching smear from where she must have brushed against the hearth when she'd poked up the coals. She certainly couldn't meet her mysterious caller in such a state of dishevelment.

Quietly, she peeked into the corridor. It was empty, thank goodness. Luck was with her, and she encountered no one as she hurried down to the end and nipped up the servants' staircase. She really oughtn't to use the smaller stairs, but it was a much faster—and more discreet—method of gaining her room than using the main staircase.

Far less chance of encountering her stepfamily on the way as well. Ever since Papa's death, it was easier to avoid them than bear their spite. The few times she'd encountered maids in the stairwell, they'd stood respectfully aside. Ellie pretended not to see the pity in their eyes or hear them whispering about how dreadful it all was.

Back in her room, she washed her face and repinned her bun, taking care to tuck away the loose strands. There was no time to change her gown—and at any rate, she had nothing but dreary mourning dresses crowding her wardrobe. Whoever was calling upon her must take her as she was.

CHAPTER 2

LORD CHRISTOPHER NEWLAND tugged up the collar of his coat and tried to ignore the clammy chill seeping into his bones. England was ridiculously cold, even in May. In Assam, it was already hot, winter clothing packed away and the edge of monsoon season on the horizon. He'd forgotten how chilly his homeland was. And damp. He turned to stare absently out the rain-spattered window of Viscount Tremont's parlor.

The late Viscount Tremont, that was. Christopher was sorry he'd not returned to England in time to call upon the man while he was alive. He had recollections of a rotund, jovial fellow who had always treated him kindly, even when he and the viscount's daughter, Eleanor, got into scrapes together. Which was often.

But at least he might pay his respects to Ellie. He was glad of the excuse to see her—and not only because he planned to return to India with a wife. He'd always been fond of his childhood companion and hoped she might still harbor some warmth toward him, despite the passage of time.

"Kit?"

He turned, recognizing Ellie's voice immediately, and the smile of greeting on his lips died. She looked dreadful.

Of course, it had been nearly six years since he'd seen her —but this pale young woman with bruised-looking eyes was a far cry from his memories of golden, laughing Eleanor Tremont.

He strode forward and took her hand, noting how very white her fingers were against his sun-browned skin. "Yes, it's me. It's so good to see you, Ellie, though I was sorry to hear of your father's passing. Are you well?"

Clearly, she was not, but he didn't know what else to say. Although her father had been gone for over seven months, she was still garbed in mourning. The black crepe of her dress made her pallor even more pronounced, and his heart squeezed in his chest to see the unhappiness in her eyes.

She cast her gaze to the carpet and carefully removed her hand from his.

"I am well enough, considering. Thank you." She waved to a pair of armchairs. "Would you like to sit? I can ring for tea."

"I can't stay." And honestly, he wasn't sure he wanted to. This sad young lady was not the girl he'd been hoping to see. "I just came by to offer my respects."

It had been foolish to expect to find the sunny companion of his youth, especially given the circumstances. A young woman plunged deep in mourning was hardly a suitable candidate for matrimony. With regret, he mentally crossed her name off the top of his list.

The charming, adventurous Ellie Tremont—the girl who might have accepted his suit and gladly accompanied him to India—was gone.

"Ellie!" A stern-looking woman with gray-shot dark hair

stepped into the room. She, too, was dressed in mourning, but the severe black and white suited her. "Whatever are you doing, entertaining a gentleman caller alone? I thought you were better bred than that."

A flush rose in Ellie's cheeks, two spots of color that quickly faded.

"I am sorry, my lady." She bobbed an apologetic curtsy. "I was about to ring for the maid. Allow me to introduce Mr. Christopher Newland. We knew each other as children. Or, wait, is it lord now?"

"Yes—now that my father is, rather unexpectedly, the new Marquess of Kennewick." He gave her a gentle smile.

Luckily, his older brother—who'd never liked India and preferred to remain in England—would inherit the burden of that title. Still, their father and mother would have to return to London for a time, leaving Kit in charge of their interests in Manohari.

Which was why time was of the essence. He must find an agreeable wife and make the journey back to India before the heaviest rains set in, rendering travel nigh impossible.

"A pleasure to meet you, my lord." The widow extended her hand so that Kit could bow over it. "I am Lady Tremont. I must apologize for whatever poor welcome Eleanor might have given you. This household is usually better mannered than that."

Despite his irritation at Lady Tremont's rudeness toward his old friend, Kit dipped his head. "Mourning can be a difficult time. I understand completely. It's a pleasure to meet you, Lady Tremont, and do forgive me for intruding. However, I must be off."

The viscountess gripped his hand, allowing him no retreat.

"Certainly not. You must meet my daughters before you go."
She turned to Ellie, her voice hardening. "Go fetch your stepsisters. At once."

As if she were nothing more than a servant, Ellie nodded
and hurried from the room. Brows furrowed, Kit watched her
go. Something did not seem right in the Tremont household.

Paying no attention to his reaction, Lady Tremont pulled
him over to the settee and all but forced him down beside her.
"Tell me about yourself, Lord Christopher. How you are
acquainted with the Tremont family?"

There was an avaricious light in her eyes, but Kit had dealt
with grasping mamas before—particularly since his father had
inherited the title. He explained to Lady Tremont the schol-
arly bond between his and Ellie's fathers and how the two
families would often visit one another with their children in
tow—especially after Ellie's mother died.

"Then you see her as somewhat of a sister, I imagine," Lady
Tremont said, a complacent note in her voice. "How kind of
you to call upon her. As you can see, her father's death has
affected us all terribly. Luckily, my fortune is large enough to
sustain us in comfort. Alas, poor Ellie has no dowry."

He frowned at her words, and not only because it was
tasteless to bring money into a conversation with a new
acquaintance. Without a marriage portion, Ellie was now
doubly disqualified from his list of prospective brides. While
he did not need an heiress, per se, it was essential he marry a
girl with a sizable dowry.

"I'm sorry to hear that," he said.

Indeed, it was surprising news. Despite his somewhat
eccentric nature, Viscount Tremont had always seemed
sensible about managing his estate. It must have been a blow

to Ellie to discover she had no dowry. No wonder she seemed so downcast.

Lady Tremont leaned forward. "If your families were such great friends, why have we not met you before?"

"My father accepted a position with the East India Company. When I graduated from Eton, I joined him in Assam."

And a happy change that had been. In addition to finding India quite to his tastes, Kit had discovered a talent for organization that was indispensible as he helped his father with various ventures. The most recent, a tea plantation in the fertile highlands, promised to be a rousing success once the bushes were ready for harvest.

But with his father unexpectedly inheriting a marquessate, the management of the plantation was now in Kit's hands. He took that responsibility quite seriously—and not only because it would make or break their fortunes abroad.

A commotion at the doorway served as a welcome distraction from Lady Tremont's interrogation. Kit rose as two young women—presumably the widow's daughters—entered the room. Ellie trailed behind them, a pale shadow.

"My darlings." Lady Tremont stood and held out her hands. "Come meet our distinguished guest, Lord Christopher Newland."

Her daughters joined her, one on each side. Neither of them were in mourning. In fact, they each wore bright colors that seemed to relegate Ellie to the background even more.

The girl to Lady Tremont's left sported a yellow-green gown that accentuated her red hair—natural red, not stained with henna, as Kit was used to seeing. She gave him a curious look, her brown eyes wide with interest.

The other daughter wore bright blue and was dark-haired, like her mother, with the same disdainful tilt to her nose. And the same appraising expression, as though weighing Kit's value to determine whether he might be advantageous to her in some way.

"This is my eldest, Delia," Lady Tremont said, nodding to the dark-haired girl.

Delia curtsied low, clearly deciding he was worthy of her favor. "A pleasure to meet you, my lord."

Lady Tremont indicated the redhead. "And my other daughter, Abigail."

"A tremendous honor, indeed." Abigail dropped him an even deeper curtsy, then shot her sister a gloating look, as though it had been a contest of some kind and she'd emerged the victor.

"Charmed to meet you both," Kit said. "I hope in the future I might become better acquainted, but, regrettably, I must bid you farewell. I've an appointment with my father's solicitor."

Which was true—although the meeting wasn't for some hours yet. But this visit had taken an uncomfortable turn into marriage mart territory, and he had no intention of adding Ellie's stepsisters to his mental list of prospective brides.

"Oh, I'm so sorry to hear that, my lord." Redheaded Abigail fluttered her lashes at him.

"Indeed." Lady Tremont's tone was dry. "As you're a long-standing friend of Ellie's, we'd be delighted to further our acquaintance. When might we expect you to call again?"

He glanced at Ellie, who stood a pace behind her step-mother. While he had little interest in getting to know the other girls, his conscience gave a twinge at the obvious unhappiness in her eyes. She needed friends, and it seemed clear there was not an overabundance of warmth between her and her stepfamily.

She glanced up at him, and he thought he detected a hint of entreaty in her expression.

"The day after tomorrow?" he asked, somewhat impetuously. It was only for old times' sake, of course. One more visit, and his duty would be discharged.

"That would be lovely," the widow said. "We shall look for you in the afternoon. And would you stay to dinner?"

"Please say yes." Dark-haired Delia stepped forward. "I would simply *adore* hearing of your travels abroad."

"Indeed." Abigail nodded vigorously and moved up beside her sister. "I've no doubt they're utterly fascinating."

Behind her stepsisters' backs, Ellie's brows rose, and she gave him the slanting look he recalled from childhood—the one that meant trouble lay ahead. Her face was transformed: a twinkle of mischief in her eye, the slightest lift to her lips. It was a welcome change, and he didn't mind that it was at his expense.

"I would be delighted to dine with you," he said.

It seemed he was willing to endure what promised to be a dinner full of dreadful attempts at flirtation if it would banish the shadows from Eleanor Tremont's eyes. *Only because we are long-standing friends*, he told himself.

And while he searched for a suitable bride, he could spare an afternoon to make Ellie smile. Happily, his father and mother were in good health, but he could imagine the devastation he'd feel if one of them passed. Poor Ellie had lost not one, but both of her parents.

"Splendid," Lady Tremont said. "We shall expect you at five o'clock on Thursday."

"Thank you for visiting," Ellie said, finally moving forward to face him. "It was good to see you again."

"Of course." He smiled at her.

"We mustn't keep you, my lord," Lady Tremont said briskly. "Allow me to see you out."

She stepped in front of Ellie, took his arm, and steered him toward the door. Ah, well. Lady Tremont might be the most maneuvering mama in London, but he was in no danger of falling into her snares. There were meddlesome mothers aplenty in India—in Calcutta, of course, but even in his home station of Manohari. He'd learned to watch his step, moving as carefully as a mongoose in a garden full of cobras.

Under the widow's watchful eye, the butler gave Kit his hat and gloves, then opened the door. Kit unfurled his umbrella. The rain made a gentle, almost friendly patter over the surface.

"Good day, my lord," Lady Tremont said. "I know I speak for my daughters as well when I say we very much look forward to seeing you again."

"Of course." Kit wondered if she included Ellie in that reckoning. Probably not.

As he turned down the sidewalk, he glanced at the parlor window to see Delia and Abigail pressed close to the glass. Abigail waved furiously while her sister lifted her hand and gave him a demure waggle of her fingers.

Ellie stood off to one side. She tilted her head and shot him another pointed look, which made him grin. Plainly, there was little love lost between her and her stepsisters—and from what he'd seen, he could hardly blame her. Dinner on Thursday might be awkward, but he'd no doubt it would be equally entertaining.

CHAPTER 3

"Did you see that?" Abby clasped her hands under her chin and twirled about. "He smiled at me!"

"It wasn't at you, ninny." Delia gave her a withering glance. "Obviously he was looking at *me.*"

Ellie bit her tongue and said nothing.

It was curious how quickly she'd felt the old childhood rapport with Kit rekindle; as though they'd just come in from a bit of mischief, like catching frogs to frighten the maids or sword fighting with sticks in the hayloft. They'd been a pair of rapscallions, as his mother had put it. And oh, how Ellie had missed him—missed his whole family—when they'd left for India.

But now he was back, and a lord into the bargain. She wasn't sure how she felt about that. Yes, it had been kind of him to pay a call, and even kinder to agree to come to dinner, but would his new station preclude them from becoming friends again? And even if it did not, was there any hope her stepmother would allow that to happen?

It had been marvelous to see him, though, Ellie had to

admit. She felt as though a crisp wind had blown in, pushing away the haze of sorrow she'd been stumbling through. He'd nearly made her laugh, and she couldn't recall the last time she'd felt that way. Certainly not since Papa died. She was glad he was coming to dinner in two days, even if it meant he must endure the fawning attentions of her stepsisters.

"Girls," Lady Tremont said, returning to the parlor and giving her daughters a stern look. "Contain yourselves. There is nothing a gentleman finds more unbecoming than a lady who has obviously set her cap for him."

"But, Mama—" Abby began.

"You in particular, Abigail, must learn to curb your emotions. Lord Christopher is a catch, no question, but subtlety will win the day, my darling."

Ellie folded her arms, an unhappy knot forming in her stomach. Of course Lady Tremont wouldn't allow a friendship between the stepdaughter she detested and the son of a marquess. And she wouldn't rest until one of her own daughters had managed to snare him into a betrothal.

A fate Ellie wouldn't wish on *any* gentleman, let alone Kit.

The only way to save him from Lady Tremont's machinations would be to pretend she had no interest in renewing their friendship. When he came to dinner, she must be cold and distant. She must extinguish that spark of camaraderie between them.

The thought made her throat tighten with dismay, but there was no other option. Kit Newland must depart her life again, for both their sakes.

"My lady." Mr. Atkins bowed from the parlor threshold. "An invitation just arrived. I thought it advisable to inform you posthaste."

He held out a silver salver bearing a letter opener and a cream-colored envelope. The seal of Queen Victoria was prominently displayed on the creamy vellum, and Abby gasped audibly.

"A royal summons, Mama! How thrilling."

Lady Tremont took it with every evidence of calm, but her eyes gleamed with excitement. She slit the envelope and pulled out a card embossed with the royal coat of arms.

"*The Lord Chamberlain is commanded by The Queen*," she read, "*to invite Lady Tremont and her daughters to a Costume Ball evoking the reign of Charles II on Friday the thirteenth of June at half past nine o'clock. Buckingham Palace.*"

"What fun," Abby exclaimed. "I do hope Lord Christopher is invited as well."

With a pleased expression, Lady Tremont set the invitation back on the salver. "We must visit the modiste at once to have our ball gowns designed."

"I will look well in a Stuart-inspired gown," Delia said smugly.

"Does that mean we are out of mourning?" Ellie asked, glancing down at her dark skirts.

The requisite six months had come and gone, but she'd been so shrouded in despair she hadn't given any thought to putting off her blacks.

Her stepsisters, however, had only worn mourning for the first month, "to spare the expense of an entirely new wardrobe," Lady Tremont had said.

For herself, Ellie had only been allowed three new mourning gowns and then was given the cast-off clothing of her stepsisters with the expectation she would alter them to fit. Never the most skilled seamstress, she had admittedly not done her best work with the alterations. It was difficult to sew a fine seam when one's vision continually blurred with tears.

"I don't believe *you* were invited to the ball," Delia said, lifting her nose. "You're not Lady Tremont's daughter by blood."

"I am by marriage, however," Ellie retorted, her fingers curling into her palms. "And I'm certain my godmother will support me in this, now that she's returned from the Continent."

Sadly, Baroness Merriweather was a rather absent, as well as absent-minded, woman. She had been an old family friend on Ellie's mother's side—thus her role as Ellie's godmother— but after Mama died when Ellie was young, the baroness became more of a myth than a matronly figure in Ellie's life.

She would resurface every few years, bringing some impractical trinket from abroad and remarking on how much Ellie had grown, then disappear again without notice. But her last visit had been only a few months ago, to offer her condolences. And she *had* told Ellie to ask if she needed anything.

Whether or not she would remember that offer was another question, but it was past time for Ellie to assert herself within the Tremont family once more. She would carry the shadow of grief for Papa in her heart forever, but seeing Kit had reminded her that life continued. The sun rose, the earth spun, and it was possible to smile again.

On no account would she let her stepfamily spoil that for her or bar her from attending social events on some flimsy pretext. No matter how much Lady Tremont might try.

Her stepmother sniffed in displeasure. "No doubt Lady Merriweather has better things to do than listen to your groundless complaints, Ellie. Let me remind you that stubbornness is very unbecoming in a young lady."

"Still." Ellie lifted her chin. "I am a daughter of this household."

True, if unfortunate," Delia said quietly.

Lady Tremont's nostrils flared. "Very well. I decree we are no longer in mourning for your dear departed father, God rest his soul. And you may attend the Queen's Ball."

"Thank you—"

"*If* you manage to procure something suitable to wear. I'm sure I needn't remind you that there is no money to furnish you with a costume. But I'm sure with your sewing skills, you'll be able to make a very fine ball gown."

Delia tittered, and Abby laughed as well, though at least she had the decency to muffle her giggle behind one hand. The remark stung, as it was meant to, and Ellie felt embarrassment warm her cheeks.

"I will be ready," she said stiffly.

Though truly, she had no notion of how she would manage to come up with an elaborate Stuart-era costume in under three weeks. Still, she refused to be daunted.

It seemed she must pay a call on Lady Merriweather and ask her to be true to her promise to help. Whether she remembered giving it or not.

CHAPTER 4

KIT PAUSED before the front door of the Tremont household and glanced down at the bouquet he carried. Pink peonies and white roses. He meant it for Ellie, of course, and had been hoping to find daisies and cornflowers, having a recollection of her weaving flower crowns from the fields.

But those blooms were not yet in full season, and at any rate he suspected Lady Tremont would turn up her nose at such a common bouquet. He also suspected that the widow would dislike seeing him pay particular attention to Ellie, and much as he relished the idea of tweaking the viscountess's feathers, he worried that Ellie would suffer the consequence.

So he had settled on a lovely, impersonal posy of flowers for the entire household. With a single daisy hidden in the center, much against the wishes of the florist. Kit hoped Ellie would understand the secret reference.

"My lord." The butler opened the door. "Welcome. The ladies are expecting you in the drawing room."

Kit nodded and surrendered his hat and coat. He followed the man down the wide hall, bypassing the smaller front parlor, and was ushered into a much grander room. Tall windows let in the light, accentuating the yellow-and-white color scheme of the drawing room. A pianoforte took up one corner, and Lady Tremont and her daughters were arranged, as carefully as flowers, in the center of the room.

His gaze went to Ellie, seated off to the side. To his relief, she no longer wore stark black, but a gown of soft lavender. Still somber, of course, but the color did not highlight her pallor—though it did echo the shadows beneath her eyes.

"Good afternoon, ladies," he said with a bow, presenting his bouquet to Lady Tremont. "Your house is already filled with sweet blooms, but I hope you'll accept my humble offering."

"You are too kind." The viscountess glanced at the flowers. "Ellie, take those and fetch a vase. We can display them on the table, there."

Ellie nodded, rising, and Kit had to bite his tongue on his objections. Why was she letting her stepmother treat her like a servant? On the other hand, if she were the one to handle the flowers, perhaps she might see the daisy hidden among the blooms. He hoped it would make her smile.

"Thank you," she said to him, taking the bouquet and not meeting his eyes.

"Do hurry," the dark-haired Delia said. "We don't want them to wilt. Such a thoughtful gift from Lord Christopher should be treated with care." She gave him a coquettish smile.

"Oh, yes," Abigail added, not to be outdone. "It's a truly magnificent bouquet."

He should have brought them daisies and cornflowers after all, just to dash their expectations—although he had the unsettling notion that he could do no wrong in their eyes.

Ellie, however, was another matter. She hurried out of the room, and he resolved to find an opportunity to speak with her privately. The warmth he'd felt between them the other day seemed to be gone, and he wanted to know why.

Was she in trouble? Did her stepmother mistreat her, beyond the obvious relegation to servant status? He wasn't sure what he could do to intervene, as a single gentleman taking rooms at Claridge's, but surely there must be a way to extricate her from the situation, if it were untenable.

In India, beneath the bright blue sky, things were much simpler. In truth, he felt a little at sea, thrown into the upper strata of Society in London. He'd navigated it well enough, he thought, until now. But what did a lord do if he suspected trouble within a household that was, on the surface, none of his business?

A pity there was not enough time to post a letter to India and receive a reply in return. His mother would know what to do—but in her absence, he must muddle along as best he could. *Your heart has ever been a true compass*, she told him as he boarded the ship to England. *Steer by it.*

And so, he would do his best. Even if the currents of the *ton* were deep and treacherous.

Lady Tremont rose from her place at the center of the sofa.

"Please sit," she said, waving to the vacant spot between her daughters.

"Thank you." Kit shot a glance at the safe bulwark of the nearby armchair.

Unfortunately, it would be rude to snub the lady's daughters so openly. With an inward sigh, he settled between Delia and Abigail, then had to resist the urge to rub his nose.

Each girl wore perfume, their scents competing instead of complementing one another. Delia smelled as though she were drenched in jasmine, and a nose-stunning overabundance of violet wafted from Abigail.

"Did you receive an invitation to the Queen's Ball?" Abigail asked. She bounced up and down a bit, clearly excited at the prospect.

"I believe so," Kit said, recalling that an envelope embossed with the royal seal had arrived just that morning.

"Will you be in attendance, my lord?" Lady Tremont asked as she settled in the chair across from him, her cool tone a subtle reprimand to her daughter.

"I intend to, yes."

The ball would be an excellent opportunity to further winnow the field and settle upon the perfect candidate for a wife. He wouldn't say such a thing aloud, of course. Lady Tremont and her daughters needed no further encouragement along such matrimonial lines.

"Have you planned to come as any particular figure from the era?" Delia asked, leaning toward him. "The Duke of Richmond, perhaps? I had thought I might emulate Lady Frances Stuart. She was known as a great beauty."

If Kit recalled his history, the two had married, despite the lady in question being desired by the king.

"I'd not given it much thought," he replied. Indeed, as the invitation was yet unopened, he'd been unaware the ball had a particular theme.

"Do consider it," Delia said, looking up at him from beneath lowered eyelashes. "The duke was such a dashing figure."

"Oh, but he died tragically," Abigail said. "I think you'd be better served as a courtier."

"I'm certain Lord Christopher will take your suggestions under advisement," the viscountess said. "Ah, Ellie, there you are. My, what a long time you took to arrange the flowers."

Ellie set down the cut crystal vase of blooms, the delicate pink of the peonies echoing the color in her cheeks. Kit suspected that whatever length of time she might have taken with the flowers, her stepmother would have found equal fault.

He surveyed the bouquet, seeing no hint of daisy petals among the blooms.

"Do you like my flowers?" he asked Ellie directly.

"Of course," she said, moving to take the armchair. "It's very kind of you."

Her answer was frustratingly vague. Then again, he could scarcely expect her to have worn the daisy openly, even if she had discovered it.

"We were just discussing the queen's costume ball," he said. "Do you have plans to attend as any particular personage?"

The color in her cheeks deepened, and Delia let out a titter.

"I'm certain Ellie will attend as someone appropriate," Lady Tremont said. "Now, Lord Christopher, how long do you intend to remain in London?"

"I plan to return to Assam by the end of June," he said. "I'll be managing my family's tea plantation there while my father comes to England to take up the duties of his new estate."

"Oh, that's a shame," Abigail said. "A month is scarcely long enough to get to know you before you leave again."

"I am of the opinion that the measure of a gentleman can

be judged within a meeting or two," her mother said, arching a brow. "And I believe you, Lord Christopher, are quite worthy."

Of marrying either of her daughters—the implication was clear.

Kit swallowed. "Most kind of you, Lady Tremont."

He sent Ellie a somewhat panicked glance. A faint, mischievous smile crossed her lips, gone so quickly he suspected he was the only one who saw it.

"Tell us about your home in India," Ellie said. "I understand the climate is rather warmer than what we are accustomed to in London."

He gave a solemn nod. "It's true. Imagine the hottest summer day here in England. Now multiply that by a factor of one third, add a host of stinging insects, and a general sense of ennui that can be difficult to overcome, and you have a June day in Assam."

It was an exaggeration, of course, but he was gratified to see Delia's mouth turn down in distaste.

"It sounds a bit challenging," she said primly.

Abigail, however, was not so easily put off.

"Surely there are Englishwomen who brave the climate for the sake of their families," she said. "Your mother has lived there for years after all."

"True, but it has been difficult for her," he lied. Then he mentally shrugged and heaped more untruths upon the first. "She can scarcely wait to return to London—especially since her lady's maid was bitten by a cobra just this spring."

"How dreadful," Lady Tremont said, casting an anxious glance at her daughters.

"It's a dangerous country, between the poisonous snakes

and diseases, not to mention the flooding and landslides caused by the monsoon rains each year." He shook his head. "In truth, it's a wonder so many English manage to carry on—especially in the wilds of Assam, which is where our plantation is located."

Ellie gave him a wide-eyed look. "But surely you are not so far from civilization as all that?"

"We manage to visit Calcutta a few times a year," he said truthfully, neglecting to mention that the town of Sylhet was much closer and provided all the basic amenities.

"It sounds very exciting," Abigail said, clearly undaunted. "And if one is in love, I imagine such things are no obstacle."

Her mother gave her a sour look. "Most matches are made for practical reasons, my dear. You'd do best to remember it."

"I don't care if my husband is titled or rich," the redhead said, tossing her head. "I intend to marry for love."

With those words, she leaned toward Kit, giving him a moon-eyed look that left no doubt as to the object of her affections. Unfortunately, he could not shift away from her or he'd be too close to her sister. It was a sticky situation.

"Don't be a ninny, Abby," Delia said. "Marrying for love is the outside of foolishness. I'm certain Lord Christopher would agree that practical matters such as breeding and fortune should be the foremost things to consider."

Her words hit a bit too close to the mark, and he gave her a strained smile. "I think practical romanticism is the best way forward."

At any rate, it seemed to work for his parents, whose strong affection for one another had helped them weather any number of tribulations. Of course, when they'd married, neither title nor wealth had come into play. It was only now, with the marquessate hanging over their heads, that such things took on importance.

"Speaking of gentility," Lady Tremont said, "may we entertain you with some music, my lord?"

"Certainly," he said. "I don't have much opportunity to hear the pianoforte. The tropical climate is hard upon the instrument."

"Girls," the viscountess said, "do the honor of entertaining our guest, if you will." She turned to Kit with a self-serving smile. "Delia plays the pianoforte and Abigail the violin, and they both sing delightfully. My daughters are very talented."

"I don't doubt it," he said.

Ellie coughed into her hand and would not meet his eyes— a sure sign that he needed to brace himself for the concert to come.

CHAPTER 5

THE SISTERS ROSE, taking their suffocating perfumes with them, and Kit pulled in a cleansing breath. Delia seated herself upon the piano bench, while Abigail took up the violin resting in a silk-lined case.

Forewarned by Ellie's reaction, he managed not to flinch as the younger sister drew the bow across the strings, producing a sound like an ailing cow.

"You're not on pitch," Delia snapped from her place at the piano. She tapped one of the keys relentlessly. "Here's the note. No, higher than that. Wait, that's too high! Go lower."

Finally, Abigail managed to get the instrument in some semblance of tune, and they launched into their first piece. Kit guessed that Abigail did not play often, as she struggled through the music. At least the pianoforte produced a pleasant enough sound, though Delia had a tendency to hit the keys with too much force.

It was difficult to discern, but he thought they were performing a Bach minuet. Thankfully, it was a short selection, and he applauded vigorously at the end, relieved it was finished.

That turned out to be just the beginning, unfortunately.

His only consolation as the sisters warbled unsteadily through a rendition of "The Last Rose of Summer" was that Ellie was clearly biting her cheek to keep from laughter. He shot her a pained glance, and her gaze skittered away from his.

Just as well. He knew they could easily set one another off, and no matter how untalented Delia and Abigail were, it would be too rude to dissolve into laughter during their recital.

It did not escape his notice that Ellie was not asked to contribute. If he recalled correctly, she had a clear, light soprano and an adequate mastery of the keyboard. No doubt Lady Tremont wanted no competition for her daughters' so-called talents.

Finally, the butler summoned them to dinner, and the caterwauling came to a blessed end.

"What do you think, my lord?" the viscountess asked, clearly proud of her offspring.

"That was an entirely memorable concert," he replied. "Your daughters have no equal." Though not quite in the direction she thought.

Ellie's mouth was screwed into a fierce frown—no doubt to hide her smile.

"That scowl is most unbecoming, Ellie," Lady Tremont said to her. "May I remind you that jealousy is unladylike in the extreme."

"You are correct," Ellie said, clearly attempting to master herself. "Do forgive me."

"Breeding will show," Delia said, rising from the piano bench and smoothing her skirts. "Lord Christopher, would you be so kind as to escort me in to dinner?"

Which was, Kit thought, rather an ironic breach of etiquette.

Her sister shot Delia a poisonous look, but the viscountess gave a regal nod.

"Indeed," she said. "Dinner is waiting. Please, follow me."

She led the way out of the drawing room. Kit followed with Delia clutching his arm, leaving Abigail and Ellie to bring up the rear.

At least Ellie was seated where he could see her, though with Delia on his left and Abigail directly across from him, he'd have to be mindful not to show her any particular attention. Lady Tremont presided over the head of the table, of course. She kept the conversation firmly fixed on her daughters throughout the meal, extolling their needlework, dancing, and impeccable taste in fashion.

This last was said with a sneering look at Ellie, and Kit quickly turned the topic to the food.

"This is an excellent roast," he said. "I've missed having beef as a regular part of my meals."

"Do they not have cows in India?" Abigail asked.

"Yes—but they are sacred beasts, and not for slaughter or eating," Kit said.

"How barbaric," Delia said with a patronizing sniff.

Ellie glanced at her stepsister. "I rather imagine that we are the barbaric ones in their eyes."

"Well put." Kit smiled at her—he couldn't help it.

"What else do you eat, or not eat, in India?" Abigail asked. "I never imagined foreign customs would be so fascinating."

He would wager she'd never given much thought to the world beyond London. Well, if nothing else, perhaps this conversation would broaden her mind a bit.

"Curries, of course," he said. "And there's a great deal of spice in all the food. It takes some getting used to." He did not add that, as a result, the food in England seemed quite bland.

Ellie sent him a glance, as if reading his thoughts. "It must be rather a change for you."

"I'm enjoying reacquainting myself with British cuisine," he said.

Well, perhaps *enjoying* wasn't the right word. He looked forward to returning to the pungent and flavorful meals of India.

"We have a lovely blancmange for dessert," Lady Tremont said.

"A fitting end to the meal," he said, keeping his tone serious. "White pudding. So very English."

Ellie twitched, and once again refused to meet his eyes. He smiled internally to see her reaction. At least her mood had lightened, which made him doubly glad he'd come that evening.

As the servants removed the plates, the viscountess turned to him. "When might we have the pleasure of your company again, Lord Christopher?"

A pity his harrowing tales of India had not discouraged her from foisting her daughters upon him.

"I've quite a bit of business to attend to in London," he said. "I really can't say."

"At least we'll see you at the Queen's Ball, won't we?" Abigail gave him a longing look.

"Assuredly." He glanced over at Ellie, partly to avoid giving Abigail any encouragement and partly to see Ellie's reaction.

She did not seem excited at the thought of the ball—not in the way her stepsisters were. In fact, her expression had teetered into melancholy. He was once more reminded that something was amiss in the Tremont household, and resolved to have a private word with Ellie before he left that evening.

"How unfortunate that you have no female relations to accompany to the ball," Lady Tremont said to him. "A bachelor arriving alone to such a prestigious event is always cause for comment. Queen Victoria and Prince Albert do like to see their subjects surrounded by family."

Clearly she was angling for an offer of escort, but he was not willing to go quite so far. He glanced once again at Ellie, noting the bleakness in her eyes.

"I hope you'll save me a dance," he said.

Although his words were directed at Ellie, both Delia and Abigail fastened upon them.

"Of course, my lord," the dark-haired sister said. "I would be delighted."

"May I put you down for the first waltz?" Abigail asked.

Her mother gave her a quelling look for being so forward, but Kit was amused by her lack of subtlety.

"Certainly," he said. "And a polka set for you, Miss Delia. They still dance the polka at balls in London, do they not?"

"Most assuredly," Delia said, somewhat stiffly. "I would be delighted, my lord."

The narrow-eyed glance she sent her sister made it clear she wished she'd spoken sooner and claimed the waltz instead.

"I shall mark you down for the quadrille, if I may?" Ellie said.

"Please do—though you might have to steer me through some of the moves."

Thankfully, he had a few weeks to brush up on his dancing skills before the ball. They did not, as a general rule, perform the more elaborate choreography at the informal dances held in the Manohari Assembly Rooms.

I must admit," Ellie said, her eyes holding a spark of amusement, "it has been some time since I attended a ball myself. I was hoping you might guide me."

"We shall invent our own steps, then." Kit grinned at her.

"I assume you are jesting," Lady Tremont said in a reproving tone. "I would not like to see you make a fool of yourself on the dance floor, Lord Christopher."

"Oh, he's far too graceful for that," Abigail said. "I can hardly wait for my waltz with you. It was so kind of you to ask."

Kit's brows rose. It seemed the redhead had already come up with her own version of events.

"Shall we retire for a few hands of cards?" Lady Tremont asked, rising.

It was more a command than a question, of course. They all stood, Delia taking a possessive grip upon Kit's arm, and obediently followed the viscountess to the drawing room.

He tried to sit next to Ellie but was outmaneuvered by her stepsisters. For the rest of the evening, he found no chance to have a word alone with her. Lady Tremont was vigilant as a hawk, and her daughters were too fixed upon him for any opportunity to arise.

At last, as he was preparing to take his leave, he caught Ellie's eye.

"Do you still ride, Miss Tremont?" he asked.

"Yes," she said, fingering her skirts. "But not recently."

"Mourning does take its toll." Lady Tremont gave an unconvincing sigh. "At least we are now emerging from its pall. But I'm afraid Eleanor has far too much to do to go gallivanting about on horseback."

"A pity," he said, keeping his tone light. "I hear the weather tomorrow is clearing at about two in the afternoon. At any rate, I thank you for a most inspiring evening, Lady Tremont."

"It was entirely our pleasure," she said with a satisfied look. "Until the Queen's Ball, my lord."

"Until then." He bowed over her hand, then Delia's, then Abigail's.

When he came to Ellie, he squeezed her fingers lightly, and she returned the pressure in two quick pulses. Good—she'd understood his message.

Whether she could contrive to escape the prying eyes of her stepfamily remained to be seen. But Eleanor Tremont had ever been a resourceful girl, and he trusted her to prevail.

The thought enabled him to smile at the gathered ladies one more time before he donned his hat and stepped into the cool English night.

CHAPTER 6

"Oh, gracious," Abby exclaimed as the door closed behind their visitor. "Just think—Lord Christopher asked me to waltz with him!"

"Ninny," Delia said. "You were the one who asked *him.* Very unladylike of you, I must say." She reached over and pinched Abby's arm.

"Ow!" Abby jerked away from her sister. "You're only jealous because he obviously prefers my spirit of adventure. Anyone could see how frightened you were when he spoke of the dangers of India."

"Why, I—"

"Girls," Lady Tremont said in a stern voice. "There is to be no more bickering over Lord Christopher. Whichever one of you he chooses, the whole family will be the better for it. The son of a marquess after all! Why don't you concentrate on *his* qualities instead of your own?"

"He has wonderful green eyes," Abby said with a sigh. "Perhaps our children will have his eyes and my hair—wouldn't that be a stunning combination?"

"You wouldn't want to curse any child with that red," Delia replied. "Dark hair is so much more becoming—which is why Lord Christopher and I would make a far better match."

She plumped her coiffure with a self-satisfied smile.

Ellie bit her tongue and tried not to think of Kit or his future; but as her stepsisters rhapsodized about his broad shoulders and ruggedly handsome face, she could not help but add her own mental comments to the list.

Kind, as he had ever been. Perhaps too kind, as his offer of dancing with them at the Queen's Ball demonstrated. Though she had to admit, it did add to her anticipation of the event.

Intelligent, with a wry humor that still matched her own. Several times during the course of the evening, she'd had to bite the inside of her cheek to keep from laughing aloud at some of his sly jokes.

Adventurous, of course. It was plain that India suited him. And she knew she shouldn't have encouraged him in his wild tales of that country, but it had been such fun seeing her stepmother's expression sour with disapproval.

It was a pity that by the end of the evening, Lady Tremont had overcome her reluctance. She seemed perfectly happy at the thought of sending either of her daughters off to face the dangers of a foreign land, as long as it would earn her the social cachet she coveted.

As if Papa's title wasn't enough!

Ellie tamped down her spark of temper at the thought. There was no use feeding her anger at her stepfamily. She knew it was a conflagration that would ultimately consume her if she let it rage forth.

But what was she to do?

Pondering that question dampened her mood completely.

Now that she was emerging from mourning, it was clear there were very few options open to her.

No dowry, and no useful connections, now that her father was gone. Perhaps someone might marry her for love, but that was a foolish notion indeed. She had no callers, except for Kit —and he was departing back to India in less than a month's time.

She was relegated to a status of unpaid servant in her own home. And although she supposed she ought to be glad to have a roof over her head and no fears about when her next meal would arrive, it was no way to exist. Especially given the spiteful natures of Lady Tremont and Delia, who were glad to belittle her at every opportunity.

Perhaps Kit would have some insight for her, provided she could slip out on the morrow. He'd been quite clever with his clues. First the daisy, which grew in a meadow in Hyde Park where their families used to picnic on warm summer days, and then his invitation to go riding and comments about the weather clearing at two o'clock. She knew precisely when and where to meet him.

Whether or not she *should* was another matter, of course— but she would bring her maid, Henderson, along. There could be no accusations of impropriety, should their meeting be discovered. Despite her resolution to keep him at arm's length, she found that the prospect of having a friend to confide in, just once, outweighed all other considerations.

HYDE PARK WAS LOVELY—FRESH, green, and sparkling from the morning's rain. Ellie drew in a deep breath as she walked beneath the oak trees. The little lane was peaceful, the grasses starred with tiny daisies. The air brightened ahead, the trees opening up to a clearing where she and Kit's families used to take picnics on warm summer days. She tried not to hasten as she and Henderson came closer to her destination, though her pulse began to pound.

It was good to be out, even if it wasn't simply to take a refreshing stroll between her shopping errands, as she'd told her maid. Henderson was circumspect, and as one of the household's long-standing servants, she was loyal to Ellie. She had known Kit's family, too, and had never liked the fact that Papa had remarried—though of course she would never say so.

"Is that Christopher Newland?" the older woman asked as they approached the meadow and caught sight of a figure waiting beside one of the tallest oaks.

"Yes," Ellie said. "You won't say anything, will you?"

Henderson frowned. "If it were anyone else, miss, you know I would. Don't do anything foolish now."

"I only want to talk to him." Ellie couldn't help the pleading note in her voice.

"Aye, well." Henderson's expression softened. "I expect it's no bad thing to speak with the lad. Just mind your manners."

"I shall."

They reached the edge of the trees, and Kit looked up, smiling. "There you are. I was worried you wouldn't be able to meet. Hello, Mrs. Henderson. It's good to see you. You look as well as ever."

The matronly woman bobbed her head. "May I say the same, my lord? India seems to agree with you."

It was true. Kit had seemed to grow into himself while

abroad. He carried himself with an easy confidence, and though his manner was still direct, he was not as easy to goad into saying rash things as he'd used to be. Which, upon reflection, was probably a good thing, despite Ellie's attempts to provoke him at dinner last night.

"It does agree with me," he said. "I'm eager to return to Assam."

"Well, then." Henderson nodded to a plain wooden bench in the shade. "I'll just rest here while the two of you have your chat."

Suiting action to words, she marched over and settled herself on the bench, appearing completely disinterested in whatever Kit and Ellie had to say to one another.

"I'm glad she hasn't changed." Kit offered his arm. "We can stroll around the clearing—staying within eyesight, of course."

"Of course." Ellie slipped her arm through his, resting her gloved hand on his forearm.

"You've changed, though," he said, giving her a keen glance. "Is everything all right, Ellie? Beyond the obvious, I mean."

She hesitated. Despite the fact that she so badly wanted someone to confide in, was Kit Newland the right choice? Perhaps she ought to seek out someone else.

But the sad fact of the matter was, she had no one else. After Papa's remarriage, the family had begun socializing with the new Lady Tremont's set, cutting ties with former friends. And Ellie's godmother was too scattered to be any kind of confidante.

"Come now," Kit said. "There's nothing so bad that you can't tell me. Whatever it is, I'll do my best to help. Is Lady Tremont mistreating you?"

The concern in his voice brought Ellie perilously close to

tears. It felt like ages since anyone had truly cared about her well-being.

She swallowed, grateful the edge of her bonnet shaded her eyes. When she'd mastered herself, she looked up at Kit.

"She doesn't beat me, if that what you mean," she said. "I'm not in any physical danger."

She paused, thinking of how to frame her words, and Kit pressed her hand, waiting. The wind ruffled the green leaves overhead, as if in reassurance.

"It's just that, with Papa gone and no money left for me, I'm relegated to a lesser standing within the household."

"I saw that." His voice hardened. "And I didn't like it one bit. They shouldn't treat you as anything less than the daughter of a viscount. You're not a servant, Ellie. You don't have to do your stepmother's bidding."

Oh, but she did, or Lady Tremont would make her life even more miserable.

"I think . . . I ought to take a position as a governess." There, she'd said it aloud, which made the possibility seem more real.

"A governess?" Kit frowned. "You can do better than that."

"Better, how?" Bitterness flared within her. As a man, he'd no notion how few options were open to her. "It's not as though I can board a ship to India to make my fortune or take a position as secretary to a lord with a promising career in politics."

"But you could marry him," Kit said, in what he no doubt thought was a sensible tone.

"I cannot. Not without a dowry."

"But surely any man can see your worth."

"That's not reasonable, Kit. You know it as well as I.

Respectable gentlemen don't marry girls of good breeding without money or connections. They have so many other choices, you see." She let out a resigned breath. "Perhaps a paid companion would suit me better."

"Nonsense." He turned to face her. "You're pretty; you've a good mind and an even disposition. What man wouldn't want you?"

Their eyes caught and held, even as warmth flooded her cheeks. He thought she was pretty? The air seemed to shimmer between them, his green eyes full of promise.

Perhaps . . . perhaps there was another option.

He *had* wanted her to meet with him after all. And he'd visited twice within the span of a week. Was it possible— could he care for her the way she always had for him?

Heart racing, she forced herself to ask the question.

"What about you? Would *you* marry me, Kit?"

His gaze slid away from hers. "I'm sorry, Ellie. You know I like you very well. But . . ."

She stepped back, her heart plummeting. Oh, she'd been an idiot to ask. She forced herself to speak through the tightness in her throat. "You see? No one will have me, despite all your fine words to the contrary. Clearly, I have little to recommend me."

"That's not so." He caught her hand. "I confess, when I first came to call upon you . . . Well, you can guess the direction of my hopes. But the sorry truth is, I must find a girl with enough money to keep the tea plantation from going under."

She blinked, trying to take in what he was saying. Had he just implied he'd been considering courting her?

"But doesn't your father's new estate have plenty of funds?" she asked.

"That's just it." Kit let out an unhappy laugh. "The marquessate is in wretched shape. The estate has been mismanaged for years, apparently, and it's going to take what's left of father's money—plus considerable loans—to make it prosperous again."

"Then why insist on this plantation? It seems clear your family can't afford both."

He shook his head, a glint of desperation in his eyes. "If only we'd known in advance. But almost all our savings is in the ground of Assam in the form of several thousand tea plants, plus the men to care for them. And the tea won't be ready to harvest for another three years. We're trapped, frankly."

Unwilling sympathy moved through her. Despite his appearance of freedom, Kit was as bound by his circumstance as she was. Oh, but life was cruel and miserable, to bring them both to this unhappy point.

"I'm sorry," she said. For everything that might have been, and could never be. "I'm sorry there's nothing we can do for one another."

"Can't we still be friends?" He searched her eyes. "I care for you, Ellie."

She knew, deep in her heart, that she and Kit would have suited one another as husband and wife. As lifelong companions. If only Papa had left her with a dowry.

It was too painful to stand with him in this clearing so full of happy memories of their youth, and see everything she'd most wished for turned to ashes.

She pulled her hand from his and turned away. "If you hear of a governess position, do let me know. At any rate, I need to return home."

He came and walked beside her. "I'll see you out of the park, at least."

"No need." She made her tone brisk. "Henderson and I can manage perfectly well on our own."

He touched her arm. "Remember to save me a dance at the Queen's Ball."

"Very well."

She would—and then she would say goodbye forever and do her best to forget that their lives had so narrowly missed being entwined.

Pretending her throat wasn't choked with misery, she bade him farewell and left him standing in the clearing, the green boughs of the oaks whispering empty promises overhead.

CHAPTER 7

"LADY MERRIWEATHER WILL SEE YOU NOW," the Baroness's elderly butler said, returning to the formal parlor where he'd deposited Ellie.

She gave him a stiff nod and rose, then glanced at Henderson, who remained perched on the settee.

"I'll await you here," the maid said. "You don't need an audience to meet with your godmother, after all."

"Thank you." Ellie gave her a grateful smile.

For the second time that week, Henderson had staunchly stood by Ellie on her clandestine visits. First with Kit, and now to beg for help from her godmother.

Despite Ellie's best efforts with a needle, she was no closer to having a costume for the upcoming ball, and time was quickly running out. Lady Merriweather was her last hope.

The butler showed her to a room full of exotic displays: a huge Chinese vase filled with peacock feathers, a marble statue of some Caesar or another, an ornate screen inlaid with gemstones. In the midst of it, the baroness sat, a writing desk on her lap. She was garbed in a bright blue walking dress accented with a tasseled fringe, and her coiffure boasted ostrich plumes dyed to match. In her right hand, she held a quizzing glass. When she looked up at Ellie, her right eye was alarmingly magnified.

"Ah, Eleanor," she said, lowering the glass. "My, don't you look peaked. Bone broth—that's just the thing." She pointed the quizzing glass at her butler. "Send up a cup of broth for our guest. And lemon tea for myself."

"Madam." The man bowed and departed the room before Ellie could protest that she had no need of cosseting.

Not to mention she despised the flavor of bone broth.

But there was no use for it now. Pulling in a breath, she went to her godmother and curtsied.

"Good afternoon, Lady Merriweather. It's kind of you to see me."

"Pish—you're family after all, even though you almost never call. Come, sit." She patted the armchair beside her own.

Ellie refrained from pointing out that the baroness was seldom at home, let alone open to receiving visitors, and took a seat. The chair was uncomfortable, the arms carved like mermaids so that there was not a smooth surface for her elbows to rest upon. Instead, she gripped her hands together in her lap and tried to find the words to begin.

"Spit it out, girl," the baroness said. "Clearly you've come to ask me for something, and there's no point in beating around the bush, as they say."

"I . . . yes. You offered your help after Papa died—and so I've come to ask if you might assist me with procuring a ball gown."

"A ball gown? Surely you have plenty of those, not to mention the wherewithal to procure more as you desire."

The quizzing glass came up again. "Unless your dear step-mama is being troublesome about money. Ah, I see that she is."

Ellie tried not to squirm. For an absent-minded old woman, her godmother was disconcertingly observant and direct—qualities Ellie admired, when they were not fixed so keenly upon herself.

"I don't know if I told you," Ellie continued, "but Papa left me no dowry. We're living on Lady Tremont's money."

Lady Merriweather's lips tightened so much that they nearly disappeared from the force of her disapproval. "No dowry? Rather suspicious, that. Your father wasn't a fool about money. Are you certain the solicitor informed you correctly?"

"Yes."

Though in truth, Ellie's raw grief had prevented her from entirely following the details. It had been a difficult meeting, full of Lady Tremont's coldness and the solicitor's apologies.

"Hmph," the baroness said. "Well, be that as it may. What kind of gown are you in need of?"

"A Stuart gown, for the queen's costume ball."

Her godmother blinked. "You plan to attend that foolish fete? The *ton* prancing about, pretending to be in Charles Stuart's court. Really! He was a naughty king, you know. Not at all a fitting candidate to inspire a ball."

Heat rose in Ellie's cheeks. Even if Charles II had run an unsuitable court, one didn't speak of such things. Except, apparently, unless one were Lady Merriweather.

"It's what the queen has chosen," Ellie said. "And our household is invited. It's the first ball I'll be allowed to attend after coming out of mourning, and I do want to go." If for no other reason than to see Kit one last time, and bid him farewell.

"And you have nothing to wear." The baroness shook her head. "It's rather short notice to procure a costume gown, my girl. You should have planned ahead."

"I was trying to make my own," Ellie admitted.

Her godmother let out a bark of laughter. "I suppose you have as little talent with a needle as your mother. Hopeless, she was. She disguised it with the clever use of sashes and ribbons and the like, though. Made it seem as though her gowns had been completely refurbished, when in fact it was her own resourcefulness with a bit of trimmings. That was before she married your father, of course. Afterwards, she could have as many new dresses as she liked."

The story kindled a warm ember next to Ellie's heart. She had so few memories of her mother that every bit of information was a gift.

"So you'll help me?" she asked.

"I can make no promises. Ah, here's Prescott with our beverages. Set the tray down, my good man." She patted the lacquered table next to her chair.

The butler complied, then departed as quietly as he'd come. With a satisfied look, the baroness handed Ellie a heavy stoneware mug. A slightly sweet, unappetizing odor drifted up from the cloudy liquid.

"Drink up," her godmother said, lifting her own porcelain cup of tea.

Ellie could hardly refuse, as she was there begging favors. Trying not to wrinkle her nose in disgust, she forced herself to take a swallow.

The cloying taste stuck to her teeth and tongue, and she must have made a face because the baroness let out a guffaw.

"Oh, child, it might taste dreadful, but it is very good for you. Like so much of life. You must steel yourself and pass through unpleasantness, but there's a reward at the end, I promise you."

"Yes, my lady."

There was no other response Ellie could make, though she was inclined to doubt her godmother's promises. Both of a reward at the end of unpleasantness and of a Stuart ball gown. But at least she'd tried.

CHAPTER 8

As EXPECTED, the week passed and no gown arrived for Ellie. She chastised herself for hoping and redoubled her efforts to cobble together a suitable costume. The days were slipping by at an alarming pace, and the Queen's Ball was imminent.

The closer it came, the more Ellie's stepfamily found every excuse to heap work upon her. From dawn till dusk, it seemed she was needed—to run to the milliner's, to consult with her stepsisters on their gloves, to rearrange the gowns in Lady Tremont's closet, as she refused to let the maids do it, claiming they wouldn't take proper care.

All of it was designed to keep Ellie far too busy to create her own costume. They didn't say as much, of course, but it was quite clear.

Despite the fact, they pretended to "help" with her ball gown, bestowing upon her various odds and ends, as if they would make any difference.

"Here," Delia said, handing Ellie a length of unused gold ribbon, frayed on the end. "I won't be needing this. Perhaps you could use it on your gown." Beneath her syrupy-sweet tones, there was an undercurrent of laughter in her voice.

"You may take this shawl." Abby tossed a length of scarlet fabric at her. "There's a tear on one edge, but if you wear it folded, no one will notice."

Even Lady Tremont participated, giving Ellie a pair of embroidered dancing slippers. "These are too small for me, but I'm certain they'll fit you. You have my permission to wear them to the ball."

As it turned out, the slippers were tight on Ellie's feet as well, pinching her toes quite painfully. But her other shoes had been dyed black or given to her stepsisters when she'd gone into mourning, so the too-small slippers were all she had. Every night, she attempted to stretch them out, but they remained stubbornly petite.

The ribbon and scarf, however, she was able to put to good use. Heartened by Lady Merriweather's remembrances of her mother, Ellie switched her focus from sewing a new gown to transforming one of her mourning gowns into something worthy of the ball. She snatched bits of time to work on her costume, staying up late into the night and working by the light of a single candle.

At least the frenetic pace kept her from thinking too much about Kit. Her childish dreams had been well and truly trampled, and there was no point on dwelling on them—no matter how much her heart ached to think on what might have been. Life had turned out differently, for both of them, and she'd do well to accept that fact and move on.

They were friends. Nothing more. And perhaps even less. Ellie had worn her heart on her sleeve at their last meeting, and he hadn't even noticed the depth of her feelings.

Enough, she told herself and concentrated on tacking the gold ribbon around the neckline of her made-over gown.

As the days passed, the severe black dress transformed. She consulted the engravings in the history books in the library, doing her best to emulate the square-cut lines and full sleeves of the Stuart era. Finally, two days before the ball, Ellie felt she'd managed to produce a satisfactory costume.

It wouldn't hold a candle to her stepsister's bespoke gowns, of course, but there was an elegant simplicity to the dress that suited her.

Finally, the day of the Queen's Ball arrived.

The last time she would ever see Kit.

For he would marry a lady with money. No doubt he was courting her even now. They would wed, and he'd take her back to India to raise a family and a crop of tea.

And that would be that.

High time Ellie turned her mind to the practicalities of becoming a governess. As soon as the endless labor of preparing for the ball was ended, she must find herself a position. Perhaps Lady Merriweather would help—though Ellie had to admit that was a bedraggled and forlorn hope. Clearly, there was to be no ball gown, and she doubted her godmother would bestir herself overmuch to help find a place for Ellie.

Then one of the maids knocked at her bedroom door to tell her she was wanted in Delia's room, and the day exploded into a whirlwind of activity.

"Which necklace should I wear?" Delia demanded, waving at the jewelry spilled across her dressing table. "You must help me decide."

It was not as simple as that, of course, because every suggestion Ellie made was countered with reasons why that particular item would not suit. There were no earbobs to match. The color would clash with Delia's underskirts. And so on, until Ellie's jaw was clenched tight with frustration.

Just as Delia finally settled on her choice, Abby dashed into the room.

"Oh, Ellie, there you are! Come tell me which combs I should put in my hair this evening." She grabbed Ellie's hand and towed her out the door.

At least Abby wasn't nearly as fussy as her ill-tempered sister. She and Ellie even laughed together as one of the feathered hair ornaments refused to stay in place.

"I don't fancy looking *quite* so much like an ostrich," Abby said, pushing the offending plume out of the way.

"More reminiscent of a cockatoo, I think," Ellie said. "Here, let's try it in this direction."

In the end, Abby abandoned feathers altogether in favor of white silk flowers that set off her auburn hair beautifully. But there was no time left for Ellie to attend her own preparations before dinner.

As the family ate, she tried not to glance too often at the clock upon the dining room mantel. The minutes ticked away; each lost moment a lead weight dropped upon Ellie's heart. Sinking. Sinking.

At last Lady Tremont set down her fork, signaling the meal was at an end.

"The carriage will be drawn up at nine," she said to her daughters. "I expect you to be ready promptly. We don't want to keep Lord Christopher waiting to claim his dances."

"But how will we find him in the crowd?" Abby asked. "Surely it will be a dreadful crush."

"I've no doubt he will locate us," her mother said. "After all, how could he not be drawn to two of the most lovely young ladies in London?"

Abby tittered, and Delia looked smug. Ellie lifted her chin and tried to pretend she hadn't been slighted once again.

"Oh, Ellie, it's too bad you aren't coming with us," Delia said, her voice sweet but her eyes sharp. "Shall I say farewell to Lord Christopher from you?"

"There's no need," Ellie replied calmly. "As it happens, I have a suitable gown."

Lady Tremont's expression hardened instantly. "I find that difficult to believe."

"Nevertheless, it's true." Ellie met her stepmother's stony gaze. "I am coming to the ball. Now, you must excuse me. There's not much time left for me to prepare."

Before her stepmother could reply, Ellie rose and hurried from the room. She ignored Lady Tremont's call for her to stop and didn't slow her pace until she'd reached the safety of her bedroom.

There, she closed the door and leaned against it a moment to let her racing pulse slow. Goodness, it had felt good to assert herself. Along with putting aside her mourning clothes, she vowed to continue pushing away the haze of sorrow that had made her so malleable to her stepfamily's demands.

Sorrow and, if she were honest, despair that Papa had left her nothing. But the fact that she had no dowry didn't mean she ought to be treated as a servant.

And . . . She drew in a wavering breath, trying to catch hold of the truth.

It also didn't mean that Papa hadn't loved her with all his heart.

Tears pricked her eyes as she realized how the notion had

shadowed her ever since his death, the insidious thought that if he'd cared for her more, he wouldn't have left her in such straits.

She closed her eyes and forced herself to breathe past the tightness in her chest. Inhale, then exhale.

Papa had loved her, and wanted everything good for her. The knowledge unfurled in her heart like a flower opening to the light, and she couldn't believe she'd let herself lose sight of the fact. He had loved her. A tear slipped down one cheek, and she wiped her eyes on her sleeve.

Whatever unlucky turn his fortunes had taken, he certainly hadn't meant it to happen, and had no doubt been distraught at the fact.

But there was no changing the fact that he had left her penniless. Her task now was to go bravely into the future, not spend the rest of her life as a dejected orphan in her own home.

And the first step was to don her costume and attend the Queen's Ball, showing the world that she was out of mourning and ready to carry on.

She rang for Henderson, who was aware of Ellie's late nights working on her costume and stood at the ready to help her prepare for the ball. With the maid's help, Ellie would manage to be ready on time . . . she hoped.

Thank goodness the ball gown was simple, as was her chosen coiffure—a bun over each ear, dressed with leftover pieces of the gold ribbon.

"There you are," Henderson said, fastening a garnet choker about Ellie's neck. "You look lovely, I must say. It's good to see you in colors again."

"Thank you for all your help." Ellie turned and pressed the

maid's hand. "I don't know what I'd do without you. I'll miss you when I go."

"Go?" Henderson's eyes lit up. "Have you heard from Lord Christopher, then?"

"No." Ellie swallowed, trying to ignore the spike of pain at hearing Kit's name. "I only meant when I obtain a position as a governess elsewhere."

The older woman's expression fell. "As to that, perhaps whatever household you go to would be in need of a chambermaid too. I wouldn't want to stay here without you, Miss Ellie."

"We shall see what turns up, then." Ellie tried to give her a cheery smile. "I'd be glad of a friend, wherever I land."

It was doubtful, of course, that they could find such a situation—and even if they did, she suspected Lady Tremont would not give a good reference to any servant leaving her household. But there was no use borrowing trouble, at least not tonight. On the morrow, she would face up to the difficulties ahead.

Henderson consulted the pocket watch pinned to her bosom. "You'd best hurry. There are only five minutes to spare."

Hastily, Ellie jammed her feet into the tight slippers and snatched up her reticule. She paused to give Henderson a quick kiss on the cheek, then, taking her skirts in both hands, hastened down the main staircase to the foyer.

The ball awaited.

CHAPTER 9

ELLIE'S STEPFAMILY was gathered in the foyer below, opulently dressed and coiffed for the ball. They turned to watch as she descended the stairs. The looks of surprise on Abby's face and envy on Delia's were gratifying, but the narrow-eyed stare of Lady Tremont sent a shiver down Ellie's back.

Still, her stepmother could not keep her from attending.

"What a singular costume," Delia said. "A pity it doesn't match our gowns. You'll look like a raven among peacocks, I'm afraid."

It was true that Ellie's somber colors were quite a contrast to Abby and Delia's pastel garb, but she wasn't overly concerned. The white silk overskirt she'd added to her gown —the lining taken from a moth-eaten woolen cloak—along with the gold and scarlet touches, transformed her costume from dreary black to an understated elegance.

Abby, as usual, was more effusive. "But how clever! I never would've guessed you could do it, Ellie. Look—there's bits of my scarf."

"And my ribbon." Delia gave her a dark look. "I wish I might take it back from you."

She took a menacing step forward, fingers crooked as though she were planning to rip the ribbon from Ellie's dress.

"Delia," Lady Tremont said. "No need to be so undignified. Ah, here comes the blackberry cordial I sent for. We could use a bracing sip before we go out, don't you think?"

One of the maids hurried up, a decanter of the dark liquid and four small goblets balanced on a tray. Just as she arrived, Delia stepped forward, knocking against the girl.

The maid lurched, the decanter of cordial swaying perilously. Lady Tremont snatched it up and then, looking Ellie right in the face, tipped it over onto her gown.

Ellie yelped and jump back, but it was too late. Sticky purple-black liquid splashed over the white overskirt of her costume, staining it instantly.

"What a clumsy thing you are," Lady Tremont said, turning to the maid. "Clean this mess up at once."

"Milady." The girl bobbed a frightened curtsy and scurried away, the empty goblets rattling on the tray.

"Oh no, Ellie," Abby said, genuine distress in her voice. "Your dress is ruined."

Ellie wanted to protest that it wasn't so, that she could still go to the ball, but the tight knot in her throat prevented her from saying a word. She could not deny that Abby spoke the truth.

"Unfortunate." Her stepmother's tone held an undercurrent of triumph. "It seems you won't be joining us after all. I'm afraid we can't linger, however. Girls, the carriage awaits."

Delia gave a satisfied sniff and turned to follow her mother, but Abby lingered a moment.

"I'm so sorry," she whispered. "I'll give your regards to Lord Christopher, shall I?"

Ellie, lips pressed together to keep from sobbing, managed a nod.

Then they were gone, and she was left standing in a puddle of blackberry cordial, her hopes for the evening as ruined as her permanently stained gown.

KIT ARRIVED PUNCTUALLY at the Queen's Ball. That is, he *meant* to arrive on time, but he hadn't realized that the line of carriages would extend so far down The Mall. After a quarter hour where they moved forward perhaps five yards, he knocked on the window of the cab he'd hired and told the driver to let him out. It would be easier simply to walk, despite the impediment of his ornate, full-skirted coat and somewhat ridiculous bloused sleeves.

At least his hose-clad legs were unencumbered. As he strode toward the palace, overtaking several carriages, he wondered how the gentlemen of the Stuart court had kept their shins warm in winter.

It was a temperate enough evening for a stroll, however. The Mall bordered St. James's Park, which breathed green and silent in the London dusk. Kit savored it. If the carriages were any indication, Buckingham Palace would be packed tighter than the crowds haggling for bargains in the morning market-place of Sylhet.

"Lord Christopher!" a voice called out as he passed a nondescript black coach.

He glanced at the open window framing Abigail Tremont's

head. Part of him wanted to act as though he hadn't seen her and hasten his steps, but the rest of him wondered how Ellie fared. She'd been much in his thoughts since their meeting in the park, and he felt guilty at how quickly he'd brushed off her suggestion that they marry.

At the very least, he owed her an apology, even if he had very good reasons why they could never make a match.

"Hello-oo!" Abigail waved frantically at him, and he could no longer pretend he hadn't seen her.

He slowed his steps and moved closer to the carriage, trying to catch a glimpse of Ellie.

"Good evening, Miss Tremont," he said to Abigail. "Are you looking forward to the ball?"

"Oh, so much." She batted her eyelashes at him. "Our dance, most particularly."

Kit simply nodded, not wanting to encourage her. Someone inside the carriage spoke, and she turned her head a moment, nodded, then looked back out at him.

"Would you like to come up with us?" she asked.

"Is there room?" he asked doubtfully. The only thing worse than going at a snail's pace would be simultaneously enduring being smothered by four sets of voluminous skirts.

"Sadly, Ellie's not with us," Abigail said, then her voice brightened, "which means there's plenty of space for you!"

"Ellie's not here? Why didn't she come?" he asked, a pang going through him. Was she that unhappy with him, that she would forgo the event just to avoid his company?

"There was a . . . mishap with her dress," Abigail said. "But I know she's sorry to miss the ball. And seeing you, of course. Shall we stop the carriage?"

It was a moot question, for the vehicle was already at a standstill, but Kit shook his head.

"I'm enjoying my stroll, thank you. But I'll wait for you at the entrance. I look forward to our dances."

In truth, he looked forward to discharging his duty and giving Ellie's stepsisters their requisite turns about the floor. The rest of the night would be spent in trying to muster up a spark of attraction for the handful of young women he'd identified as the best candidates for his suit.

Surely, he reasoned, there must be some warmth between himself and the woman he was to marry—especially if was carting her off to India. But so far, he'd felt nothing but a resigned sense of responsibility as he sought a bride. And time was running out.

"Very well," Abigail said. "We shall see you anon, Lord Christopher."

He nodded to her, then lengthened his stride. The remainder of his walk to the palace was spent pondering whether there was any other solution besides marrying a girl with money. Alas, no other possibility presented itself.

With a heavy sigh, Kit glanced up, wishing he could see the stars. Only the faintest spatter of constellations were visible as he passed between the gas lamps, and he missed the diamond-strewn night sky of India with a sudden, fierce yearning.

Perhaps he needn't marry after all. Perhaps he ought to return to Assam and . . .

And what? Dismiss the workers, watch the tea bushes die, and return to Calcutta to beg a position as a junior officer in the Company?

Which was worse: being trapped in marriage with a wife

he had no feelings for or seeing all the family's hope of a prosperous future wither away?

There was no answer, and dwelling on such grim thoughts was no way to spend the evening at a fancy dress ball. Even if Ellie Tremont wasn't going to be in attendance, he could enjoy himself—or at least try.

With a last glance up at the distant, nearly invisible stars, Kit stepped onto Buckingham Palace's porticoed entrance. At least, while he waited, he had an entertaining parade of nobility to watch.

Finally, the carriage bearing the Tremonts pulled up. He went forward to greet them, compliment them on their costumes, and offer his escort up the stairs. He could not help noticing that Lady Tremont looked entirely too self-satisfied as they ascended.

There was another wait at the door while the Lord Steward verified the attendees and announced their arrivals, but at last their turn came.

"Lord Christopher Newland," the man bellowed. "Viscountess Tremont and the Honorable Misses Delia and Abigail Tremont."

Abigail giggled at the announcement, then turned to Kit. "Do you think our dance will be soon?"

"I most fervently hope so," he said, though not for the reasons she thought.

Unfortunately, there were any number of presentations to the queen and prince before the orchestra struck up. The first dance was a polka, and he dutifully took Delia out upon the floor. She alternated between flirtatious looks and an artificial-sounding laugh that soon grated against his ears, but Kit did his best to be amenable. For Ellie's sake.

His waltz with Abigail was a bit easier to bear, despite her moon-eyed gazes and heavy sighs every time he guided her into a turn.

"Will Ellie be at home tomorrow?" he asked. He could not leave London without saying goodbye.

"We all will be." She gave him a bright look. "Why, are you planning on paying us a call? How delightful."

So much for his hopes of seeing Ellie alone. Perhaps they could meet in the meadow once more, instead. If he gave the butler a note, could the man be trusted to pass it to Ellie without alerting Lady Tremont?

Kit attempted to steer the conversation back toward safer ground, but it seemed Miss Abigail was determined to view everything he said as a particular flirtation toward her. Finally, he gave up and simply danced—no easy feat, considering the crowded condition of the floor.

At the conclusion of the waltz, he returned Abigail to her mother, then fled as quickly as he might. There were other young ladies in attendance he must seek out—no matter that he had little enthusiasm for the task ahead.

Indeed, there was Miss Olivia Thornton, a young heiress whom he'd met at a musicale the week before. Ignoring the heavy sensation in his chest, he went to pay his regards and ask her to dance.

He was determined to make up his mind by the end of the evening. The sooner he chose a bride, the sooner he could return to India. The rains would not hold off just because he was squeamish about doing his duty. His future—indeed, his family's fortune—depended on it.

CHAPTER 10

ELLIE HUDDLED beside the fire in her room, a thick shawl over her shoulders, and tried not to let misery engulf her. In the hour since her stepfamily had departed, she'd tried desperately to scrub out her gown, but it was no use.

There will be other balls, she told herself.

But none with Kit in attendance, and that was the bitterest blow of all, that she would not be able to say goodbye.

"Miss Ellie!" Henderson knocked on her door, her voice urgent. "There's a delivery for you."

"What is it?" Ellie rose, suddenly feeling the aches of all her labors echo through her bones.

"Just come—quickly."

When Ellie opened her door, Henderson took her by the elbow and towed her rapidly down the hall.

"A footman is waiting in the foyer," the maid said. "And if I'm not mistaken, he arrived in Lady Merriweather's coach. I caught a glimpse of it waiting outside. That color is quite unmistakable."

"The orange one?" Ellie caught her breath, hardly daring to hope.

"Yes, the one that all the gossips deplore."

"Is the baroness here, too?"

Henderson shook her head. "I don't know. Perhaps she remained in the coach."

They reached the stairs, and Ellie hastened down, Henderson at her heels. As the maid had said, an elderly footman stood near the front door. The butler, Mr. Atkins, had taken up his post and was ostensibly reading the newspaper. Between the men sat an upright trunk. Ellie's heart skipped a beat.

"Miss Eleanor Tremont?" the white-haired man asked. At Ellie's nod, he gestured to the trunk. "Your ball gown has arrived, compliments of your godmother, Lady Merriweather."

"A bit late, isn't it?" Henderson said under her breath.

Ellie sent her a quelling look, then turned back to the footman. "Did she accompany you, by any chance?"

"She did not," the man said. "But she gave strict instructions to convey you to the Queen's Ball with all haste."

"You must give her time to dress," Henderson said, giving the man a cold look.

"I won't be long," Ellie promised. After all, her hair was already coiffed, and she still wore her jewelry.

"We will take as long as is necessary," Henderson said. "Bring the trunk up to my lady's dressing room now, if you please. Follow us."

The footman nodded and heaved the trunk onto one shoulder. Little caring about the etiquette, Ellie led him directly up the main staircase. When they reached her room, he set his burden down with care, then made her a half bow.

"We await you downstairs," he said. "At your convenience."

As soon as he left, Ellie unfastened the latches, her fingers clumsy with anticipation. Henderson moved to brace the upright trunk, and Ellie slowly pulled it open.

"Oh," she said softly as the ball gown inside was revealed.

The dress was stunning. The pale blue silk of the bodice and overskirt shimmered, as though interwoven with silver threads. Rosettes of darker blue velvet lined the edges of the skirt, setting off the embroidered gold underskirt beneath. Another rosette decorated the front of the bodice, with touches of gold at the sleeves and neckline.

"My stars," Henderson said. "In that gown, you're fair to outshine the queen."

"No one can compare to Her Majesty," Ellie replied. "But it *is* a beautiful gown."

"Then let's get you into it, posthaste." Henderson lifted the dress out and laid it across the bed. "Fortunate that your hair ribbons match the gold. Oh, and look—a lace cap to go with it. That will suit perfectly."

A blue velvet bag remained, tied to a hook inside the trunk. Ellie retrieved it and found a jewelry box tucked within. Inside the box was a set of sapphires—necklace, earbobs, and brooch—and her breath caught in a sob at the generosity of her godmother.

"Heavens." Henderson laid a hand on Ellie's shoulder. "The baroness has outdone herself on your behalf."

There was a note tucked under the necklace. Ellie's eyes were too blurred with gratitude to read it, so she handed it to Henderson.

"The jewels are a loan," the maid read. *"You may return them within the week. But keep the dress—I hope it fits. Your affectionate godmother, Constance Merriweather."*

Ellie pulled in a deep breath, mastering herself with effort. There were times to dissolve into tears—but this was not one of them.

Fortunately, the dress *did* fit. A few small adjustments in the shoulders and waist, a quick pinning of the lace over her hair, the sapphires fastened on, her gloves donned, and she was ready.

"I'll accompany you in the coach," Henderson said. "We must be mindful of the proprieties, and I want to see you safely delivered to Buckingham Palace."

"Thank you." In truth, Ellie was glad of the company.

She feared her nerve would fail her, arriving so late to the Queen's Ball. But with Henderson there, she would not turn back from the intimidating thought of entering the palace alone.

True to his word, the footman waited below, with Mr. Atkins keeping a watchful eye.

"Best of luck, Miss Eleanor," the butler said. "I'm pleased you'll be able to attend the ball after all. Most unfortunate, that mishap earlier." He frowned and shook his head.

"Thank you, Mr. Atkins," she said, warmed once again by the support and kindness of the servants.

"Look after her," he said gruffly to Henderson, then opened the front door.

The footman bowed and ushered them out to where the singularly orange coach waited. Inside, it was upholstered in pumpkin-colored velvet, with candles behind glass shedding a warm illumination. Ellie climbed inside, assisted by the footman, and settled her voluminous skirts. Henderson followed, taking the seat across from her.

They did not say much during the ride. Ellie's heart hammered with fear and excitement. What would her step-mother say, to see Ellie gowned like a princess and arriving so remarkably late? Would Kit still be there? Oh, she desperately hoped so, and that she might claim one last dance with him.

Almost before she was ready, the walls of Buckingham Palace were in sight. The guards at the gate waved them through, and the coach pulled up to the Grand Entrance.

"At least there's not a crush to get in," Henderson remarked. "There's one advantage of arriving so late."

Ellie simply nodded, her throat tight with anticipation.

The footman opened the door and handed her down from the coach.

"If you find it agreeable, I shall escort you in," he said to Ellie.

"Yes. Thank you." Even an elderly footman was better than approaching that intimidating facade by herself.

"And I will find the ladies' maids and wait until the ball ends," Henderson said. "Dance well."

"I'll do my best." Ellie managed a smile.

She would not mention that her embroidered slippers still pinched her feet quite uncomfortably. A pity the baroness had not sent footwear, but, she chided herself, her godmother had been more than generous.

Luckily, the gown was a trifle long, the skirts sweeping down to trail on the ground. If Ellie removed her slippers to dance, well, no one would be the wiser.

Setting her gloved hand on the footman's arm, she entered Buckingham Palace. The red-coated guards on duty at the front door did not even glance at her as she and the footman walked between them. She supposed that was better than reproving glances on the tardiness of her arrival, though it rather did make her feel invisible.

At the long, red-carpeted sweep of the Grand Staircase, she nearly lost her nerve—but truly, she could not turn back now. Instead of focusing on her racing heartbeat, she tried to concentrate on the ornate gilded balustrade, the huge portraits of former monarchs lining the high walls.

They reached the top of the stairs, and now she could hear the crowd—a murmur like the sea, punctuated by occasional strains of music. The doors of the Green Drawing Room were open, though she could not see much of the room beyond except a few bright dresses and plumed hats. An official-looking fellow—perhaps an under steward—presided over the threshold.

"My lady," he said, stepping forward. "Have you an official invitation?"

"I was invited, yes." Ellie met his gaze. "I am Miss Eleanor Tremont, joining Lady Tremont and her daughters, who arrived earlier."

Much, much earlier. But there was nothing to do but brazen it out.

"Miss Tremont, is it?" The steward gave her a penetrating look. "I was not notified you would be coming so late. The ball is well underway."

"With all due apologies," the footman said, "she was unavoidably delayed by my mistress, the Lady Merriweather. But Miss Tremont is here now, and, as you can see, quite ready to make her entrance."

The steward raised one bushy brow. "Lady Merriweather, you say?"

"Yes," Ellie said. "She is my godmother."

The man let out a harrumph, but it seemed the baroness's reputation as an eccentric stood Ellie in good stead.

"Very well," he said. "I will announce you. Most everyone is gathered in the Throne Room, however, and will not hear you come in."

"I don't mind," she said.

"Best of luck, milady." The footman bowed over her hand.

She smiled her thanks at him, and then he was gone and the steward was announcing her name in a deep voice. It was time to step forward—in every sense of the word. Shoulders back and chin high, Ellie made her entrance to the Queen's Ball.

CHAPTER 11

IT WAS, admittedly, rather anticlimactic. As the steward had said, most of the attendees were packed into the Throne Room, just visible through the double doors at the end of the Green Drawing Room.

Ellie walked through the high-ceilinged room, trying not to wince as her slippers pinched her toes. The chandeliers shed brightness over the figured green carpet and olive-hued walls. A half-dozing elderly gentleman in one of the scattered chairs marked her passage, as did a wilted-looking young lady and her companion, but with those two exceptions, the room was strangely empty.

Noise poured from the scarlet-draped Throne Room ahead, however—a blast of music followed by the sound of applause. She edged into the room in time to see a line of costumed dancers make their bow to the queen and prince, who stood on a raised dais to one side of the crowded space.

Ellie noted with relief that Queen Victoria wore a magnificent ball gown. Intricate lace framed the neckline, and gold trimmings accented the white silk bodice and overskirts, while the underskirt was a rich, rose-colored brocade. The queen made an altogether splendid picture, especially with her equally well-garbed consort at her side.

Pride filled Ellie, that she was a subject of such a regal couple. And thank heavens she would not have to worry about outshining the monarch at her own ball.

While the dancers filed off the floor, Ellie glanced about the room, hoping to catch sight of Kit. And her stepfamily, so that she might avoid them.

She thought she glimpsed Abby's red hair in the far corner, but she couldn't be sure. Then her heart lurched as she spotted Kit making his way toward the door. He looked rather unhappy for a fellow who was attending the most celebrated ball of the Season.

"Excuse me," Ellie said, wedging herself between a woman wearing bright green skirts and a courtier in a coat that stuck out so far from his body she wondered if he'd put part of a hoop crinoline beneath.

After a brief struggle, she emerged, just in time to catch Kit's arm as he went past. He turned, and the look on his face transformed in an instant, like sunlight breaking through storm clouds. The light in his eyes made her catch her breath, and she berated herself for a fool.

Even if Kit had feelings for her, he'd made it all too clear that he would never ask for her hand.

But in that moment, with the musicians striking up a waltz and the crystal chandeliers overhead sparkling with a thousand tiny fires, she didn't care.

"Ellie," he said, the warmth in his voice unmistakable. "I thought you weren't coming."

"I was delayed," she said. "Luckily, my godmother managed to procure me a gown at the last instant."

"And a lovely one it is too. You look particularly beautiful in it."

She blushed. "You weren't leaving, were you?"

"Not any longer." He lifted his head and scanned the floor. "I know it's cramped quarters, but might I have the pleasure of this dance?"

"I'd be delighted," she said, then frowned at the thought of trying to waltz in her too-tight slippers.

"What is it? I promise not to step on your toes."

"I *am* worried about my toes," she confessed. "My dancing slippers are intolerably small."

He leaned forward. "Slip them off, then," he said in a confiding tone. "I won't tell."

"I'm scandalized," she teased. "What an improper thing to suggest."

However, she had already stepped out of the offending footwear, pushing them off each foot with her toes. The bare floor felt blessedly comfortable.

"They're already off, aren't they?" His eyes twinkled with mischief.

"Yes—except I can't bend over to pick them up." Not only was the space too crowded, she feared her skirts would fly up. She wasn't used to wearing such voluminous lengths.

"Push them to the edge of your gown, then drop your fan," he said. "I'll pick it up and collect your shoes into the bargain."

"But where can I put them? My reticule is too small."

"Leave that to me." He gave her a conspiratorial smile.

Trying not to grin too broadly in return, she let her fan fall, then scooted the slippers out from under her hem.

Kit swooped them up. Bowing, he presented her with her fan. His other hand was tucked awkwardly beneath the skirts of his coat.

"You can't simply hold them there," Ellie said. "It looks very odd."

"Take my arm, then. Your sleeves will cover them. Yes, like that."

It was ridiculous, smuggling her slippers through the crowded room, and she was on the verge of laughter as Kit maneuvered them close to one of the floor-to-ceiling windows. With one swift motion, he thrust the footwear behind the red velvet draperies, then turned to her with a triumphant look.

"Now we are free to dance."

"You're incorrigible," she said, laughing.

It felt like old times—like she had a family and friends and no worries for the future.

"And yet eminently practical." He gazed down at her with a warm smile. "You can retrieve them when you go. It's the last curtain."

"Yes, I've marked it."

"Then come—this dance won't last forever."

He deftly swung her out onto the floor, and suddenly Ellie wished it *would* last forever. She could happily spend an eternity with her hand clasped in his, his arm about her waist as they whirled in a scarlet sea beneath a thousand diamond suns.

Her pale blue skirts swung out, and anyone watching could have seen her stockinged feet—but she did not care. Nothing else mattered except this moment, waltzing with Kit —the way they used to practice in the daisy-starred meadow, when she had no cares, no sorrow chaining her to the ground.

But, as it must, the music ended, and her heart regretfully returned to earth. Kit released her, and she was conscious that her pulse was racing—partly from dancing, but mostly from being near him. The heat and jostle of the throng pressed in upon her.

"Might we step out a moment?" she asked. "I could use a bit of air."

"The Picture Gallery should be less crowded," Kit said.

"You know your way about the palace." She lifted one brow. "One might almost think you're a frequent visitor here."

He gave her an amused look. "I'm not, I assure you. I discovered the gallery as a useful retreat earlier this evening when your stepsisters were trying to cajole me into multiple dances."

"Completely understandable," she said, tucking her arm through his. "Lead on, good sir."

He wove them through the mob to the wide opening leading to the gallery. Several other guests had the same notion and were perambulating about the wide hall, but on the whole it was much less crowded.

They paused before a large painting of Queen Charlotte, and Ellie pulled in a breath. "This is much better."

"I agree—though I did enjoy our waltz very much."

"As did I." Bittersweet melancholy tugged at her heart.

She was nerving herself up to ask him when he was departing England, when an older gentleman viewing the next painting glanced over at her.

"Why, is that Miss Eleanor Tremont?" he asked, a note of pleased surprise in his voice.

"Hello, Lord Brumley." She made the earl a curtsy, recognizing him as one of Papa's old friends. "Yes, it's Eleanor."

"How good to see you, my dear—and looking well. I must say, I was sorry to hear of your father's passing."

"Thank you." And for the first time in eight months, she was able to respond without fighting back tears. "Allow me to introduce my escort, Lord Christopher Newland."

"A pleasure." Lord Brumley extended his hand. "Newland, is it? Any relation to the new marquess?"

"Yes, he's my father," Kit said.

"Will he be taking his seat in the House of Lords this fall? I understand he has connections in India. I'm rather interested in the spice trade myself."

"My father certainly intends to take up the duties of his new title," Kit said. "He plans to arrive in England within the next two months."

"Excellent. Tell him to call upon me when he reaches London. We can trade tales of our travels abroad, compare India to Indonesia and whatnot." Lord Brumley gave him a jovial smile. "In fact, why don't you pay a visit yourself, young man? Find me at Brumley House on Grosvenor Square."

"I shall, thank you."

"Now, off with you both," the earl said, waving them away with a shooing motion. "You young folk should be dancing and enjoying yourselves."

"Yes, my lord," Ellie said. "It was nice to see you again."

With a lighter heart, she and Kit continued their stroll. His company, plus her newfound ability to bear hearing condolences on Papa's death, made her feel as though she were returning to herself. No longer the grief-stricken shadow of a girl or the pliant servant of her stepfamily, but Ellie Tremont, who would face the world on her own terms.

They reached the end of the gallery, where columns flanked a small, nearly hidden anteroom. Ellie glanced at Kit.

"Is this the last time I'll see you before you return to India?"

"I expect so." His gaze met hers, green eyes the color of shadowed oak leaves, no trace of a smile on his firm lips.

As she had feared—and expected. "Will you give me something to remember you by?"

"Of course." He pressed her hand. "Anything you ask."

Her heart thumped wildly. Oh, it was daring of her, but this was her last chance . . .

"A kiss," she said softly. "Just one."

If she were fated to life as a spinster governess, she wanted a glimpse of what it would be like to share a kiss with the man she loved. A single, perfect moment to hold next to her heart and carry with her always.

His eyes widened a fraction, but he nodded. Without a word, he pulled her into the shadows behind the columns. His head dipped to hers, and between one heartbeat and the next, their lips met.

Sensation glittered through her, as though starlight were pouring atop her head and sifting down through her body in silver waves. The place where their mouths touched tingled, and she swayed forward. He caught her against his chest, and tears pricked her closed eyes at the feeling of being pressed so close to him.

It was anchor and storm all at once, safety and tempest whirling in a delicious mix through her very being.

And then it was over.

Blinking, she stepped back. His gaze fixed on hers, Kit gave her a crooked smile that seemed equal parts tenderness and regret.

"Will that do?" he asked.

No, she wanted to say. *Never. Stay with me.*

Instead, she gave him a somewhat stiff nod and stepped back into the main gallery. None of the others in the room had seemed to notice their brief absence, although she thought she saw a flutter of pastel skirts at the entrance to the Throne Room.

After a moment, Kit joined her.

"My ship sails next week," he said, a hint of bleakness in his voice.

"And what of your quest to find a bride?" The words felt like shards of glass in her throat, but she must ask.

"I believe Miss Olivia Thornton is amenable to my suit," he said, not sounding any happier than she.

Ellie swallowed. She did not know Miss Thornton other than as a very distant acquaintance. "She seems a pleasant young lady. And well dowried, I suppose."

"Yes, that." Kit shook his head, his expression strained. "Please, can we talk of something else?"

"There she is!" Delia's shrill voice cut through the air.

Ellie glanced at the doorway to the Throne Room to see her stepfamily approaching. A sneer of triumph on her face, Delia marched in the lead, followed by Abigail and Lady Tremont. Ellie curled her hands into fists, resisting the urge to turn and flee. Cold apprehension washed through her, erasing the last echoes of Kit's kiss.

"Eleanor." Lady Tremont's voice was hard. "How very irregular. You have a great deal of explaining to do."

Ellie's throat went dry as she confronted Lady Tremont's baleful stare.

"My godmother sent me a ball gown," she said, forcing her voice to remain steady. "And Henderson accompanied me."

"You should have joined us directly," Lady Tremont said. "Instead, I discover you sneaking off with Lord Christopher—"

"I asked Ellie to dance," Kit said, stepping forward to shield her. "She'd only just arrived. And then the crush on the dance floor demanded we take a moment to catch our breaths. If you must find fault, Lady Tremont, then I ask you lay it at my feet, not hers."

Delia sniffed and gave him a pointed look. "You are not the gentleman you've led us to believe, Lord Christopher."

"I never pretended to be anything other than who I am," he replied.

"Be that as it may," the viscountess said, "you are henceforth forbidden to visit our home, sir. And speaking of which, we are headed there directly. Girls, collect your things."

Ellie wanted to protest that she'd only just arrived, but the evening was well and truly ruined in any case. She moved toward the ball room to retrieve her slippers, but Lady Tremont took her arm in a tight grasp.

"No more sneaking away into corners," her stepmother said. "You'll wait outside with me while they bring the carriage around."

Pointedly turning her back on Kit, the viscountess stalked to the doorway leading into the Green Drawing Room, pulling Ellie along with her.

Ellie glanced over her shoulder, hoping Kit could read the apology in her eyes. It was a mortifying end to a night that had careened from bliss to humiliation, and it was certainly not the way she'd wanted to bid him farewell.

"Goodbye, Kit," she called.

His expression set, Kit made her a low bow, as if she were truly a princess. He straightened and their gazes met one last time.

Then Lady Tremont hustled her out of the room, and everything was gone. Her hopes. Her dreams. Her childhood friend.

Everything, except herself.

Ellie pulled her arm out of her stepmother's grip.

"I can navigate the stairs on my own," she said coolly.

Not to mention the rest of her life. On the morrow, she would pay a call on Lady Merriweather to return the sapphires—and secure her help in finding a governess position as quickly as possible.

KIT WATCHED ELLIE GO, a hot, uncomfortable knot in his chest.

He shouldn't have kissed her—he knew better—but he'd wanted to for weeks, if not years. And she *had* asked.

Unfortunately, all he wanted to do was keep kissing her. That, and sweep her off to India with him. She would thrive there, he suspected, once she grew accustomed to the climate and culture.

Tonight, he'd seen the old Ellie—the girl who'd challenged him to a tree-climbing contest and, when he'd lost, forced him to read books of poetry that he'd found surprisingly enjoyable. The girl who'd teased him into being a better person and awakened his sense of adventure. The girl he'd once known he'd marry—known fiercely, with the entire burning surety of his fifteen-year-old heart.

As Kit stood in the opulent gallery, the sounds of gaiety drifting from the Throne Room, the realization slowly crystallized within him. His younger self had been right.

He could not marry anyone except Eleanor Tremont.

If he did, he knew that, despite his best efforts, he would constantly compare whomever he wed with Ellie, and find her lacking. That was a sure recipe for a miserable marriage.

Ellie might have no dowry, but life with her was the only path to happiness he could see. For both of them, if he read her emotions aright.

He must find a way to save the tea plantation without marrying for money. True, he and his father had spent long nights turning the problem over and they had not seen a better way.

But he could not save the plantation at the expense of his own heart.

There had to be a solution—and he vowed he would find it.

CHAPTER 12

ELLIE REGARDED HER BARE WARDROBE, then glanced at the partially empty trunk on her bedroom floor. Perhaps she would fill the rest of it with her favorite books. There was no guarantee her new employer would let her make free with their library, after all.

"Must you really leave?" Abby asked from her perch on Ellie's bed. "And to take a job as a governess, of all things? I'm going to miss you."

"I know." Ellie sent her a fond glance. "But I must take this position with the Granvilles, especially as Lady Merriweather arranged it on such short notice. Please, try to understand."

"Oh, I do." Abby grimaced. "As soon as I can, I'm going to find an agreeable husband and leave the house, myself."

"Don't settle for just anyone." Ellie tucked her small pouch of jewelry into one of the trunk's pockets. "You deserve someone who will treat you with consideration."

Abby heaved a sigh. "I would much prefer love—but as Lord Christopher has been banned from the house, there's no hope of that."

Not that Kit had ever intended to offer for Abby, but Ellie kept that thought to herself. There was no need for unkindness, especially during this last hour before her employer's coach came to collect her.

"Kit has left for India, in any case," Ellie said, the knowledge weighing heavily upon her heart.

She'd hoped for a note of farewell, at least, and kept a careful eye on the mail to make sure Lady Tremont didn't get her clutches on any envelopes meant for Ellie. But the days had passed, and there was nothing from Kit.

And now he was gone.

"Miss Eleanor." Mr. Atkins rapped upon her half-open door. "You have a caller."

Sir Granville must have sent his carriage early.

"I'll be down in a moment," she said.

With a sigh, she shut the lid of her trunk. As she straightened from doing up the latches, Abby flung herself off the bed to give her a tearful embrace.

"Don't go," her stepsister said with a choked sob.

"There, there." Ellie patted her back. "I'll have one day off a week, and I'll come visit. The Granvilles don't live so far away as all that."

When they were in town, that was. She didn't mention that the family was planning to repair to their country estate for the rest of the summer. Why add to Abby's unhappiness? With her mercurial nature, she'd recover as soon as Ellie stepped out the door.

Well, perhaps not that quickly, but still.

Leaving her stepsister blotting her eyes, Ellie went downstairs. She paused before the parlor door to pat her hair into place, wondering who Sir Granville had sent to escort her.

A man stood in the center of the room. Ellie froze, heart clenching as she saw it was not some unknown stranger, but Kit Newland, grinning unrepentantly at her.

"Hello, Ellie," he said. "I wasn't sure if the butler would let me in."

With a tremendous thud, her heart resumed beating.

"It's really you?" she asked, trying to balance her careening emotions. She didn't know whether to laugh or cry—or quite how to interpret his unexpected visit. "I thought you'd taken ship already."

"Not yet," he said. "I brought you something."

He stepped forward and handed her the slippers they'd hidden behind the curtains at the Queen's Ball.

"You fetched them out?" she asked, a catch in her throat.

He certainly had no obligation to do so, and his thoughtfulness nearly undid her altogether—no matter that she despised the too-small slippers.

"Of course." He raised his brows. "It wouldn't do to leave evidence of the crime behind. This way, you can dispose of them properly."

"Please don't tell me you delayed your journey simply to bring back my slippers," she said, setting them aside.

"Not entirely." His expression turned serious. "The truth is, there's something I couldn't bear to leave behind."

Her hands trembled, and she squeezed them tightly together.

"What might that be?" she asked, trying to keep her voice steady.

"Can't you guess?" He took another step and gently set his hands on her shoulders. "My heart, Ellie. Don't you know it's in your keeping?"

She shook her head. "But . . . what of Miss Thornton and her dowry?"

"After the ball, I realized you were the only one for me. Drat it, I'm not doing this properly." He released her shoulders and went down on one knee. "Miss Eleanor Tremont, would you do me the very great favor of becoming my wife?"

She wanted to say yes—oh, how she wanted to—and yet . . .

"What about your tea plantation?" She knew she must turn him down, despite the anguish burning in her chest. "I can't let you ruin your future for me, Kit."

"I wouldn't ask you to," he said solemnly. "Lord Brumley has agreed to become an investor."

Ellie drew in a disbelieving breath. "He has?"

Kit reached and took her hands, smoothing her fingers and clasping them in his. "It took some convincing—and even more time to settle the paperwork, or I would have been here days ago—but yes, the plantation is saved, whether I marry for money or not."

"And would we live in India?"

"Is that agreeable to you?" Concern shaded his eyes.

"Yes," she said fervently. "I would very much like that. And more to the point, I would very much like to marry you, Lord Christopher Newland. Someone has to keep that title from going to your head, after all."

He gave a shout of laughter and stood. Then they were in one another's arms, and Ellie's despair turned to a brilliant, shining joy.

"What's this?" Lady Tremont's voice snapped through the room. "Lord Christopher, you are not welcome beneath this roof. I require you to leave, immediately."

"He can't." Ellie faced her stepmother defiantly. "He's my betrothed."

Lady Tremont blanched, her eyes wide with shock.

"You can't marry," she said in a voice shrill with anger. "I forbid it. Forbid it! Do you understand?"

Kit stepped between them. "Too late. And now *I* require you to cease threatening my fiancée."

"Out!" Lady Tremont shrieked, pointing toward the door. "Out, the both of you."

"Gladly," Ellie said, feeling a sure calm descend over her. "My trunk is already packed. See it delivered to Lady Merriweather's. Come, Kit."

Ignoring her stepmother's poisonous glare, she brushed past and headed for the front door, Kit at her shoulder.

Mr. Atkins held the door open, an apologetic look on his face.

"So sorry, miss," he said. "I'll send Henderson to you."

"Please do." She paused. "When we depart for India, I'll offer you a place. If that's all right, Kit?"

"Of course," her fiancé said, his hand warm at her back. "And your maid too, it goes without saying."

A loud crash from the parlor made them turn, and Mr. Atkins winced. "I'm afraid that was the Chinese urn. You'd best be going."

Ellie nodded. "Please tell whomever Sir Granville sends that I've had a change in plans."

She would have to make her apologies to that family, and to her godmother, but under the circumstances, she wagered they'd understand.

As she and Kit climbed into the cab he'd hired, another shriek of rage drifted from the house. She'd no idea why her betrothal had sent her stepmother into such a fierce tantrum, and she had no intention of returning to find out.

"Lady Merriweather's," Kit told the driver, and the man nodded.

The coach jolted into motion, and Kit took her hands once more.

"I even brought a ring," he said, a bit forlornly, "but that didn't go at all as planned."

"It was a memorable proposal, at any rate." She smiled at him, her spirits rising with every moment they traveled away from Tremont House. "May I see it?"

He drew a small velvet bag from his pocket and shook out the ring. "I had to guess on the fit."

She held her left hand out, and he slipped the ring onto her finger.

"It's perfect," she said, looking down at the yellow tourmaline surrounded by diamonds.

"The closest thing I could find to a daisy," he said with a smile.

"Absent that flower, it will have to do." Then she laughed and leaned forward to kiss him, and everything was right with the world.

IT WAS NOT, of course, quite as simple as that.

Lady Merriweather required several explanations, but at last she was satisfied and agreed that Ellie might remain with her until their departure for India.

Henderson appeared in due time, along with Ellie's trunk, which proved to contain some books and Abby's second-best pelisse. The additions made Ellie's heart warm even further toward her stepsister, and she vowed to ask Kit's parents to look in upon Abby when they arrived in England.

The most surprising development, however, came three days later, when Papa's solicitor paid Ellie a call.

Her godmother gave a nod, as though she'd been expecting such a visit, and accompanied Ellie down to the yellow parlor to meet with the man—a brown-haired fellow named Mr. Tippet.

After the pleasantries had been concluded, the solicitor set his folder of papers on the table before them.

"Now that you're to be married," he said, "we have the details of your inheritance to be worked out."

"I beg your pardon?" Ellie regarded him with some confusion from her place on the sofa. "I was given to understand that Papa left me no money."

Mr. Tippet gave her a precise nod. "True, but only until your marriage. Then you are to come into the thirty thousand pounds he left you."

The breath left her in a whoosh, and she sagged back. It was a substantial sum, and suddenly Lady Tremont's rage at hearing of her betrothal made sense.

"Excellent," Lady Merriweather said, lifting her quizzing glass. "If I might take a look at those papers?"

The solicitor pushed the neat stack her way, and she made a few *hms* and *tsks* as she paged through.

"I take it my stepmother knew of this provision," Ellie asked, the first surge of anger overcoming her shock.

"Of course she did." The solicitor blinked at her in dismay. "Do you mean to say she did not inform you? She said the news would come better from her and bade me not to speak of it."

"No." Ellie's voice was hard. "She said nothing."

So much of Lady Tremont's behavior made sense now—keeping her in mourning, treating her as a servant so that she would remain downtrodden in her own home. Telling her she had no dowry! It was the outside of enough. Bitterly, Ellie wondered how many callers her stepmother had turned away for fear of Ellie catching some suitor's eye.

"I am so sorry." Mr. Tibbs sounded flustered. "I had thought . . . that is, I assumed . . ."

"Not everyone is as honorable as you are, sir," the baroness said dryly. "However, all the paperwork appears to be in good order. Congratulations, my dear. You are an heiress."

Ellie still could not grasp it. If only she'd known! She and Kit might have married right away.

And then she would have spent the rest of their marriage wondering if he loved her more for herself, or for her money.

No. Despite the terrible enormity of Lady Tremont's lie, it had allowed Ellie and Kit to find their true way to one another, to follow the compass of their hearts without going astray.

"I imagine your young man will be glad of the news," the solicitor said. "He must think quite highly of you, if he believed, er . . ."

"That he was marrying a penniless orphan?" Ellie said tartly. "As a matter of fact, he does love me, very much. And while this is a very welcome circumstance, it will not matter to our happiness."

Lady Merriweather cleared her throat. "I assure you, it will make a difference—though I've no doubt you would have been happy either way. But it is far easier to be content in life when one has a small fortune at one's disposal. Speaking of which, I rather fancy the thought of coming to India for your wedding. Perhaps I'll be your chaperone until you're wed. What do you say to that?"

Ellie smiled at her. "I think it would suit very well."

She and Kit had decided to have the ceremony abroad so that his parents might attend—and so that her stepmother might not. After the revelations of the afternoon, Ellie preferred never to set eyes on that dreadful woman again.

"Then it's settled," the baroness said. "We set sail next Wednesday. In the meantime, I'll help you with opening bank accounts and the like. One doesn't want a sum that size sitting about in bills, after all."

"Very wise," the solicitor said. "We can meet tomorrow at the Royal Bank. Two o'clock?"

While her godmother settled the particulars, Ellie contented herself with imagining telling Kit the good news. With the investment from Lord Brumley, she had no doubt the tea plantation would thrive.

And with her inheritance, she had no doubt their family would, too. She closed her eyes a moment, conjuring up a vision—a house with a wide veranda tucked beside a prosperous tea plantation, she and Kit sitting outside, watching their children play. Two—no, three of them, a girl and two boys.

Henderson was there, and Mr. Atkins, who found the heat a blessing to his old bones. The baroness visited every few years, bringing the children strange, exotic items from England. And surprisingly, Abby would visit as well, along with her ambassador husband, who altogether doted upon her.

Through it all—the year of drought, the monsoons that washed away a third of their crop, the blight five years after that—she and Kit persevered. And, at last, found financial prosperity.

But it was nothing compared to the wealth of love and companionship they would share together till the end of their days.

READY FOR MORE SWEET Victorian romance? Pick up a copy of **Noble Holidays** *for a delightful quartet of tales that will warm your heart!*

OTHER WORKS

~ THE FEYLAND SERIES ~

What if a high-tech game was a gateway to the treacherous Realm of Faerie?

THE FIRST ADVENTURE - Book 0 (prequel)

THE DARK REALM – Book 1

THE BRIGHT COURT – Book 2

THE TWILIGHT KINGDOM – Book 3

FAERIE SWAP - Book 3.5

TRINKET (short story)

SPARK - Book 4

BREAS'S TALE - Book 4.5

ROYAL - Book 5

MARNY - Book 6

CHRONICLE WORLDS: FEYLAND

FEYLAND TALES: Volume 1

~ VICTORIA ETERNAL ~

Steampunk meets Space Opera in a British Galactic Empire that never was...

PASSAGE OUT

STAR COMPASS

STARS & STEAM

COMETS & CORSETS

ABOUT THE AUTHOR

Growing up, Anthea Sharp spent most of her summers raiding the library shelves and reading, especially fantasy. She now makes her home in the Pacific Northwest, where she writes, plays the fiddle, hangs out in virtual worlds, and spends time with her small-but-good family. Contact her at antheasharp@hotmail.com or visit her website – www.antheasharp.com and join her new release mailing list (plus get a bonus free story when you sign up!)

Anthea also writes historical romance under the pen name Anthea Lawson. Find out about her acclaimed Victorian romantic adventures at www.anthealawson.com.

Printed in Great Britain
by Amazon

42677049R00131